D1328144

ANNIE'S ATTIC MYSTERIES ®

Wild Things

Karen Kelly

Annie's ®
AnniesMysteries.com

Library of Congress-in-Publication Data
Wild Things / by Karen Kelly
p. cm.
I. Title
                    2013902407

AnniesMysteries.com
800-282-6643
Annie's Attic Mysteries®
Series Editors: Ken and Janice Tate
Series Creator: Stenhouse & Associates, Ridgefield, Connecticut

10 11 12 13 14 | Printed in China | 9 8 7 6 5 4 3 2 1

～ 1 ～

"Why did I let you talk me into this?" Alice MacFarlane muttered to her best friend, Annie Dawson, as she pulled her car into a parking space near the Stony Point Community Church.

"Because deep down you know it might be a good thing for both of us," answered Annie, reaching down to pick up a bag bulging with her yoga mat, towel, and water bottle. "It's past time for us to pay more attention to staying limber and working on our balance. Also, you're a pushover for a bribe."

Alice slung her own duffle over her shoulder and slid out from under the wheel, shutting the door behind her. "Don't forget, it has to be a *large* iced coffee." She cocked her head at Annie. "Seems like you're taking the whole 'turning fifty' thing pretty seriously. It's still out there a ways, you know."

"Just wait until you're staring its arrival in the face." Annie squinted at her friend through the bright sunlight as they walked across the small parking lot toward the white clapboard building that served as both church and community center for the small Maine coastal village. "I can't deny it's sobering, especially considering—"

Alice's voice grew serious as she continued Annie's line of thought. "Considering how your father and husband died so young. I should have remembered before teasing you."

Annie paused before continuing down the walkway to

the building, taking in the sight of the lawn and trees finally wearing lush green. "At least I have the comfort of knowing Gram and Grandpa led full lives. I'd just rather do what I can to take after them, and not my parents or husband, as I grow older. I want to stay active like they did."

Annie's grandparents, Charles and Elizabeth Holden, had both lived long, active lives. Annie had spent many childhood summer months at Grey Gables with Charlie and Betsy and knew they were both happy and healthy. Even though Annie's mother had died of tuberculosis while on a mission trip and not from a potentially genetic disease, it still left Annie with additional motivation for paying close attention to her health.

"Somehow I can't quite picture Betsy in a Pilates class," Alice said with a gentle smile. "OK, I get what you're saying." She breathed in a lungful of crisp June air before moving again toward the building. "However, I'm still going to let you buy my coffee."

The gentle breeze lifted the soft blond-gray curls of Annie's hair. "I'll even make it hazelnut, if you want."

"Deal!" They approached the large double doors of the building. Alice stepped ahead to open it, holding it open for Annie. "Age before beauty."

Annie wagged a finger at her childhood friend. "Watch it now, or no coffee for you!" She stepped over the threshold and glanced around the large open room to see where the class was meeting. Women of all ages were gathered near a stage, wearing different versions of workout clothes. A couple more women were coming in from the other end, where a kitchenette and restrooms were located.

The door closed behind Alice as she moved forward, searching the cluster of women for anyone she might know. Noticing a young blonde milling around the edge of the group, she said to Annie, "Oh, there's Sherry. No teddy-bear smock, I see." An aide at Seaside Hills Assisted Living, both Annie and Alice rarely saw her in clothing other than her uniform of printed smocks and white pants. As they drew close, the women waved to her.

"So is this how you stay so energetic for your work?" Annie smiled at the young woman in red yoga pants and a white sleeveless top.

"Hi. It's good to see you here. Is this your first class?" Sherry pulled a bright blue yoga mat from her gym bag.

Annie and Alice nodded.

"This is one of my favorite ways to relax before heading to work. You might feel awkward at first, but you'll get the hang of it fast. Trust me. Pammy's a really good instructor, so don't hesitate to ask her for help."

"If we have enough breath, we will," joked Alice. Before she could say more, a willowy woman with short-layered hair moved to the front of the group and positioned herself a few feet from the stage, centered to be seen easily. The various conversations around the room dropped off into quiet as attentions were redirected.

"Good morning, everyone!" Pammy's voice was somehow both lively and calm at the same time. "Welcome especially to our new class members or those of you taking the free trial. I hope you like what we do today. With consistency, you can expect to experience in-creased body awareness, improved posture, as well as a boost in your strength and flexibility. Does that sound good to everyone?"

Amid the general sounds of assent, one woman raised her voice, "I'm not convinced I want body awareness. It's doing some weird things at my age!" Annie glanced over at Alice, who laughed at the comment along with many others in the room.

Pammy wasn't fazed, and a rueful grin took over her face. "I hear you. But once you learn body awareness, you'll learn how to better control your muscles, and it will result in improvements in so many areas. Then body awareness won't be so scary."

"If you say so," the woman replied, not sounding convinced.

Sherry leaned over to whisper to Annie and Alice. "Pilates really does make a difference, like Pammy said. I don't get sore after a long shift at work like I used to."

Pammy instructed the class to spread their mats out in rows, making sure each student had plenty of room. "Now, we're going to start with a spine and back warm-up."

For the next 45 minutes Annie and Alice put their conversation and concerns aside as Pammy led the class through a whole-body Pilates workout. After chatting with some of the other class members, the two friends staggered out the front door.

"Who knew 'fluidity' and 'centering' would make me sweat so much." Alice wiped her face with a towel.

"I always thought my 'core' was in decent shape," Annie mused. "Now, I'll be happy to just be able to move tomorrow."

"Working in your garden will be a joy," Alice said,

snickering as she dug her keys out of her bag. "Are we going to come back again?" She opened the trunk of the Mustang and stowed her gym bag.

Annie pulled a small purse from her bag before placing it next to Alice's. "Maybe we should tackle that question after our coffee." Annie waved toward the house next door, where Reverend Wallace's wife, June, had just emerged from the church's manse. "Good morning, June!"

The gray-haired woman broke into a warm smile and hurried toward them with an empty tote bag hanging from one arm. "Hello there, Annie and Alice! Looks like you two have been exercising."

"If you mean twisting ourselves into knots and bizarre shapes, yes, we've been exercising," answered Alice.

June gestured at the bag on her arm. "I'm exercising too. By walking to the shops. Sure is a beautiful day."

"Would you like some company?" asked Annie. "At least to The Cup & Saucer. I promised Alice an iced coffee for coming with me to the exercise class."

Alice chimed in, "A large, hazelnut iced coffee, to be specific, and I earned every drop!" She tucked her car keys back in her bag. "It makes more sense to walk to the diner, if I can limp that far."

"With it being right next door, I've considered trying Pammy's class. I just don't know if I'm up to it," June said. "Throwing my back out in the pursuit of fitness would be counterproductive." The three women walked past the Town Square. It stood quiet and expectant, as though holding its breath until the children were released for summer vacation, filling it again with activity.

A slight look of remorse crossed Alice's face. "Don't let my dramatics keep you from trying the class, June. I really challenged myself with the harder versions of the positions, and so did Annie. Pammy is very good at demonstrating different levels of difficulty."

Annie laughed. "We may regret our enthusiasm come tomorrow morning, mind you. But give the class a try. That's what the free trial is for, to make sure it's a good fit for you."

They paused at the intersection of Elm and Main streets. Annie and Alice needed to cross over to the other side of Main, while June was headed for Magruder's Grocery. "Thanks for your encouragement," June said. "If you make it to the class again, you might just see me there. Enjoy your coffee … and the rest of the day!"

"Please say hello to Reverend Wallace for us," Alice called after her. She and Annie stepped off the curb, making it to the middle of the street when the loud squeal of tires startled them.

The two women sprang back toward the sidewalk, staring at the black SUV that had almost hit them as it fishtailed from its careen around the corner. The driver gunned the engine and continued down Main Street. Annie leaned against her friend. "What possesses people to drive like that?"

Alice shook her head as they watched the vehicle disappear southbound toward Portland. "Who knows? Can't blame this one on tourists, though. It had a Maine license plate."

"It looks like it's headed out of town, and I hope it keeps going!" Annie straightened up and took a deep breath. "I really need that coffee now." The women paused long enough to peer meticulously down both streets before scurrying across to the diner.

To Annie and Alice, The Cup & Saucer was like an old friend—an old friend who promised a cup of good, strong brew. As soon as they entered the diner, they spied their friend Peggy Carson behind the long counter and hurried to catch her.

"Hey, girlfriends," she greeted them, pulling her order pad from the apron covering her pink uniform. "Is it food and coffee, or just coffee today?"

"Just coffee," Annie answered.

"How fresh is the hazelnut?" Alice asked. If one looked closely, the shimmer of a wink could be detected.

Peggy's manicured nails drummed on the counter; the tiny boats on each blue nail looked like they were dancing over waves. "Well, if you're not in a hurry, I could brew you the freshest pot possible. We're running low after the breakfast rush."

"Perfect," Annie said. "An excuse to sit down before we walk back to the car. Just don't stand too close to us, Peggy. We've been at Pammy's class and are none too fresh ourselves." The two women each flopped onto a stool at the counter.

"And then some muttonhead in an SUV almost mowed us down," Alice added. "I'm sure the jolt of fear didn't help any."

Peggy slapped a hand down on the counter. "You're not kidding me, are you? I hate when that happens. But it's kind of early in the season for tipsy tourists."

"I don't think it was a tourist," said Alice. "Maine license plate and no rental car decal that I could see."

"And how many rentals do you see with dark-tinted windows?" Annie added.

"Hmmm, I hope one of Maine's finest catches up with them before they do even more serious harm to someone." Peggy began to prepare the coffeemaker for brewing the hazelnut blend. "Oh, and don't worry about your freshness. Have you been around the fish and lobster folks after they've had a hard day at sea? I serve 'em every day. One little exercise class isn't going to smell you up like that, even with a side of fear!"

"Thanks, Peggy. Oh, and we want the coffee iced!"

"Got it!" Peggy called over her shoulder as she hurried over to a booth with a pot of regular coffee, refilling proffered mugs.

Annie swiveled her stool to face Alice. "Time to put the near miss behind us. So, what do you really think of Pammy's class? Do you want to keep going?"

"Do I have to decide before I see how sore I am tomorrow?" Alice raised a dark auburn eyebrow.

"How about we assume the soreness factor won't be a game changer?" Annie suggested. "There's plenty of time to change your mind before the next class."

Alice dug into her bag to retrieve her smartphone and unlocked it.

"You need to call someone to help you answer?" Annie teased.

A soft snort was Alice's only response as she opened up a search engine and started tapping. When Annie tried to peer over her shoulder, she hunched away from her. So, Annie stared at the coffeemaker, watching as the aromatic hazelnut java dripped into the pot. When it was almost to the brim, Alice snapped the phone shut and directed her attention back to her friend.

"OK, now I have a little more information to help with my decision," she said.

"What kind of information?" Annie rested a cheek in her hand as she waited.

"Oh, things like average calories burned per session, potential hazards, chances of needing emergency chiropractic care."

"And?"

Alice paused—whether for dramatic effect or because she was being mesmerized by the act of Peggy pouring her coffee over ice, Annie wasn't sure. "I'm willing to attend at least a few more sessions. But I'm warning you, if I get bored, I'm outta there. How about you?"

Peggy placed a large take-out cup of iced coffee before each of them. "Doesn't get fresher than this."

"Why do you think we come here so much? Who else pampers us like you do, Peggy?" Annie said. Alice was too occupied with taking a deep drink to speak, so she simply slowly nodded her agreement.

"No one I know. And that includes Mr. Mayor," Peggy quipped with a wink. Ian Butler, the widowed mayor of Stony Point, had been smitten with Annie almost from the moment she first stepped foot in town after she had inherited Grey Gables. And while their relationship had weathered several challenges, those who cared about both Annie and Ian hoped it would someday flower into a Stony Point romance.

"Here comes a group of tourists," Peggy exclaimed.

"Looks like I'll be busy for a while. See you on Tuesday!" She scurried to greet the arriving customers.

Tuesday mornings were special for the Hook and Needle Club, a group of needlecraft artists that met at A Stitch in Time, a yarn and fabric shop owned by Mary Beth Brock. The club gave the women a chance to share their individual projects—and their lives—with each other. Several times a year they also worked together to provide support for various charities and benefit events.

Alice rolled her straw between two fingers. "To get back to where we were, what did you think about Pammy's Pilates?"

Annie took a small sip before replying, savoring the rich flavor. "I like your idea of committing to trying it several more times. That's a good way to get a better idea of the positive effects of Pilates."

"Or the lack thereof," added Alice.

Annie conceded to the possibility. "Yes, though I do suspect it will at least strengthen my 'core,' as Pammy called it. How could it not with all those exercises that used our stomach muscles!" She placed a hand against her middle. "Surely my waist is shrinking as we speak."

Alice leaned closer and cocked an ear toward her friend. "Hmmm, oh yeah, I can hear something. What's this?" Her voice rose to a squeaky pitch. "I think it's saying, 'Help! I've been stretched, and I can't move!'"

"Very funny." Annie whacked Alice's nearest shoulder with a rolled napkin. "Just in case, though, it might be wise to go get our warm showers before we get stiff."

With a wry look on both faces the friends waved to Peggy, who was taking orders from two men at a small corner booth. Alice paused on her way to the cashier to whisper to Annie. "Those guys don't look like the typical tourists we see in Stony Point."

Annie shifted her position so she could observe the men without being obvious. "I see what you mean. Two guys in their twenties wouldn't find much to do vacation-wise. Maybe they just moved here to work on a boat or the docks."

"I doubt it," said Alice. "They don't look like they spend that much time outdoors to me."

Annie started for the cashier again. "Well, give Peggy a little time, and she'll get their story, if there is one. Ask her on Tuesday."

"Good idea, I think I will," Alice said as she waited for Annie to pay for their coffee before they left the diner.

Standing on the corner outside, waiting for a car to pass—hesitating longer than they normally would—so they could cross the street, Annie squinted and then brushed a hand in front of her face. "Oh my, I think the iced coffee after intense exercise is affecting my vision."

"Like how? You're not going to faint on me, are you?" Alice peered at her friend's face.

Annie slowly shook her head, still staring at the sidewalk opposite them. "No, but I might be hallucinating. See that woman over there, the one in the shirtdress and sweater?"

Alice located the woman with a stylish shoulder-length cut and sunglasses with little trouble. "Yes, I see her, so you're not hallucinating. What about her?"

"She's an identical twin to a friend from back home in Texas, Seneca Marchal. A total doppelganger. But it can't be her."

"Are you sure about that?" Alice asked, as the woman lifted her arm and waved in their direction.

"Annie! Hi there!" The woman stepped to the edge of the curb, and as soon as another car passed, she hurried across toward the two women.

Annie's eyes widened, and she clapped a hand on Alice's shoulder in excitement. "I can't believe it! It *is* Seneca!"

2

As soon as Seneca stepped onto the sidewalk, Annie rushed to embrace her friend. "I can't believe it! What in the world are you doing here?" Seneca had changed little in the years that Annie had been in Maine, except for a deepening of two lines between her eyebrows. Worry lines, Gram used to call them.

Seneca Marchal was still a strikingly beautiful woman. A trim brunette with willowy brown eyes, the forty-something journalist exuded vitality. Annie had always thought Seneca breathed life into any room simply by stepping into it.

Annie's friend squeezed her tightly. "It's your fault, you know. Always writing about how lovely Maine is in June. I just had to come see it for myself." She pulled back enough to look closely at Annie. "You look amazing, my friend. Your new home obviously agrees with you."

"I'm not sure how amazing I am right now since Alice and I have just come from a workout. If it's true that women don't sweat, they glow—well I've been glowing a lot." Annie chuckled. "But as far as my new home, you're right. It's been an adventure."

"After adventure, followed by more adventure," Alice added.

Seneca nodded at Annie's auburn-haired friend. "Which is exactly what Annie needed after losing Wayne so suddenly and selling the car dealership. Something new and completely different."

Seneca had been Annie's main source of encouragement after Wayne's death—she was always there when Annie needed to talk, and she had reached out to Annie when she retreated too long into a thick shell of grief.

Annie shook herself, a gentle movement, and gestured to Alice. "Where are my manners? Seneca, this is my friend and neighbor, Alice MacFarlane. Alice and I have known each other since childhood summers when I visited my grandparents here in Stony Point. Alice, Seneca and I met when she wrote a wonderful feature article on our dealership years ago."

"Still the same modest Annie, I see." Seneca turned toward Alice. "I wrote the feature when the dealership won the Small Business of the Year award. No small honor! Then Annie and I just clicked. That doesn't happen with everyone I interview, you know."

Alice grinned. "Yes, one of Annie's most enjoyable traits is her clickability."

"How long are you staying?" Annie rushed on. "Please don't tell me you're only passing through on your way to Canada or some such."

Seneca reached a hand up to one of her dangly earrings, fingering the green and blue beads. "After seeing you and your charming town, there's no way I could leave so soon. I've taken a room at Maplehurst Inn. It's been such a busy year, I've earned some rest and relaxation time before returning to that giant oven called Texas."

Annie's green eyes sparkled. "Now, that's good news!

But, Seneca, why don't you come stay with me at Grey Gables? There's plenty of room—a big ol' house with just me and one cat."

"Even though the cat has a sizable personality, there's still an abundance of rambling space," Alice inserted.

Seneca hesitated. "Thank you for your hospitality, Annie. I would love to come see your new home, but I think I should stay at the inn. Even though I'm on vacation, my editor tends to forget and calls at strange times. I'm also in the throes of midlife insomnia, and I'd hate to interrupt your schedule with my late-night prowling."

Though surprised, Annie hid it behind her smile. "I understand, Seneca. But the invitation stands, if you should get tired of the inn, as nice as it is. I honestly don't think your editor or insomnia would bother me."

"Thanks, Annie." Seneca reached out to squeeze her friend's hand. "I would love to treat you both to dinner tonight. I can't wait to hear about all these adventures you've been having."

"Of course I'll have dinner with you, but you don't have to treat," Annie protested.

"I insist," Seneca said, "and that goes for both of you."

Alice sighed. "It sounds like fun, but I'm headed for a hot shower. I have a Princessa party tonight that I can't reschedule at this late notice. I'd much rather help Annie tell you about her mysteries." She turned to Annie. "Save a couple stories for me to tell, will you?"

"Princessa party?"

"Alice represents Princessa, a jewelry company, and has parties to display and sell their products," Annie explained. "She has similar events for Divine Décor, an interior design company."

"That must keep you busy," said Seneca. "Well, I was just heading to the grocery to pick up a few things, so don't let me keep you from your well-earned shower too, Annie. How's six o'clock for you?"

"Just right," Annie said. "I'll even wear something more stylish than yoga pants."

"You could wear an Aggies T-shirt, and I'd be thrilled just the same."

"But we'll miss you tonight, Alice," Annie said. "Can you come for lunch after church tomorrow?"

"Just try and stop me," Alice responded. "Don't make dessert, though. I want to bring it."

"Seneca, wait until you taste Alice's baking," said Annie. "She could hold her own with any of the cooks on television."

Seneca's shoulders relaxed noticeably, and her smile brightened. "Normally I don't eat baked goods much. But what's vacation for, if you can't loosen up a little on your normal diet? I'm sorry you won't be able to join us, Alice, but I look forward to getting to know you while I'm here."

"Same here," Alice said. "I need to get home soon, sadly. There's a good amount of prep work still to accomplish, and I'm in serious need of a shower after our workout!"

The ladies chuckled and walked together across Main Street, where Seneca turned toward Magruder's. In unison Annie and Alice called, "Bye!" as they turned left toward Elm.

"You never know what a day may bring." Annie shook her head in amazement. "The rascal never said a word about visiting in any of her letters."

"No email?" asked Alice.

"No." Annie paused to return a wave from Grace Emory, who was standing by the door of the Stony Point Library, and Alice joined in the greeting. "Seneca says she spends so much time at a computer for her job at the newspaper that the last thing she wants to do is email. She has beautiful handwriting too. It would be a waste if she hardly used it."

The two women rounded the corner onto Elm, into the breeze coming off the harbor. "I like her perspective," said Alice. "Actual paper and pen communication has become so rare now. Each one's a small treasure."

"Yes, they are." Annie pushed a curl from her cheek. "I told myself I'd make sure my grandchildren would experience the fun of opening a letter written just for them in my own handwriting. I love talking to John and Joanna on the phone and seeing photos and videos of them on Facebook, but nothing beats opening the mailbox to find an envelope from them with a drawing and note."

Alice dug into her bag for the car keys as they approached the parking lot. "John and Joanna are blessed in the grandma department."

"I'm blessed in the grandchildren department. And the daughter and son-in-law department." Annie and Alice paused at the curb to make sure no vehicles were coming up from Ocean Drive and then strode across the street to the lot.

Reaching the Mustang, Annie looked into her friend's eyes. They turned almost meditative. "Yes, you are blessed," Alice said. "Life's a strange mix of joy and sorrow, isn't it?"

Annie nodded as she walked to the passenger side of the

car. "I once heard a speaker say that suffering is the black velvet on which shines the diamonds of God's grace. It's taken years, but I think I understand what she was saying now." Alice unlocked the doors and Annie lowered herself into the low-slung seat.

"I can see how you have come to that place in your life." Alice slid the key into the ignition and turned it. "Me? I'm not at the place where I can embrace suffering just so I can shine more beautifully, I'm afraid." Alice backed out of the parking space and made her way onto Elm. "Does that make me shallow?"

"It makes you human," said Annie. "I don't believe God gives us the grace to handle future suffering, just grace for the needs of the present."

Alice's fingers tapped a rhythm on the steering wheel. "Hmmm, like the manna in the wilderness, eh? That's something to remember."

"Is something bothering you?" Annie glanced over to read her friend's face. "You sound ... contemplative."

"You're getting entirely too good at reading people, you know?" Alice drew in a deep breath as she turned onto Ocean Drive. "We don't have time to really hash it out right now, but I'll give you an overview."

"Fair enough." Annie drew quiet, allowing Alice the space to collect her thoughts—enough space to carry them into the driveway of Grey Gables. She relaxed into her seat to hear what her friend had to say.

Alice turned off the engine and turned to face Annie. "It's work," she said. "For a while now, I've been stuck in a rut. The job doesn't inspire me anymore, no matter how many ways I try to spice it up. I'm not sure how much longer I can work at it with zero motivation. Or what to do to improve it."

For as long as Annie had known Alice, her friend had been the vivacious one, the never-ending fount of ideas and creativity. To see her tapped out like that spread a fan of concern through Annie. "How long have you been feeling this way?" she asked.

Alice closed her eyes for a minute, like drawing drapes to block out a dazzling blue sky. "I've been really struggling for a few months, but it started at least a year ago."

"That far back?" Annie tried to stifle her gasp, so it came out sounding like a strangled hiccup. "You hid it so well! Why did you wait so long to mention it?"

Alice shrugged. "I kept thinking it would fade away, or I'd find a way to work differently that would relight the creative spark. But the sizzle has fizzled, and I'm afraid it's beyond resuscitation." She twisted in her seat to face her friend. "Annie, I'm beginning to get scared."

"That's not an easy thing to admit." Annie reached out to grasp Alice's hand. "I can't say I know exactly what you're experiencing, but I can relate to your struggle. It takes me back to my porch in Texas, rocking in a chair and feeling completely out of place in the routine I had thrived in for decades."

"Yes! Exactly." Alice's head bobbed up and down. "I can't believe I waited so long to talk to you about it."

"Well, now you have and that's what matters," Annie replied, waving a hand to shoo away the recriminations. "I can't help but think that what you're experiencing are the birth pangs of a new opportunity."

"I hope so." Alice glanced at her watch. "Yikes! I better stop yakking and get going. I have packets to make before the party. In case you hear my music cranked up, let me apologize in advance. A fast beat is about the only way I can get myself to go through the motions these days."

Annie wrinkled her nose and exaggerated a martyr's sigh. "All right, advance apology accepted." She opened the car door. "Just don't forget to bring dessert tomorrow."

A short laugh escaped Alice's lips. "I promise to make an extra-delicious one. Have fun tonight."

Telling Alice to have fun didn't seem appropriate, so Annie just nodded. "Thanks. See you tomorrow!" Annie dashed up the porch steps and disappeared into the house, as her friend backed down the driveway for the ride next door.

*   *   *   *

A couple minutes before six o'clock, Annie approached the front entrance of Maplehurst Inn. Before she could grasp the gleaming brass handle on the door, it opened, and a smiling employee greeted her. "Good evening, Mrs. Dawson."

Annie smiled her thanks as she entered the lobby of the Colonial-style hotel. "Hello, Connor. How are your classes at the university going?"

"I'm halfway through, so they must be going pretty well. Thanks. It's a lot of work, though." Connor had been working summers at the inn since he was sixteen, and Annie was pleased to see the evidence of his promotion to working in the lobby, assisting the guests in full uniform.

Annie quickly skimmed the main room for signs of

Seneca. Then she turned her attention back to the young man beside her. "A college education is a huge commitment, but well worth it. I hope you'll have some time to enjoy your summer break."

"I'm sure going to try, Mrs. Dawson." Behind the young man, Annie saw Seneca descending the wide, gracious staircase. Annie hurried across the large room as Connor was pulled aside by a frazzled mother with two young children who needed help with their luggage.

"Annie!" Seneca met her at the bottom of the stairs. "You surely clean up nice."

Annie laughed and ran a hand down the soft fabric of her floral maxi dress. "Remember when these were the latest thing in fashion?"

Seneca squinted, as if trying to see through a century of years. "Barely. Though I don't remember needing to wear sweaters with them."

"It's rather nice for a change, I think. We'll have our sweltering days this summer, but thankfully they don't tend to stick around very long." The two women made their way past the fireplace to the entrance of the dining room and paused to wait for the hostess. "We'll have to make sure to spend plenty of time walking the beach. There are few things I find more relaxing and invigorating at the same time."

"That sounds heavenly."

The hostess approached them. "Welcome to Maplehurst Inn. Do you have a reservation?"

"No," Seneca answered. "Will that be a problem?" Annie showed no response in her face, but she was surprised. Seneca was the Reservation Queen. Her friends teased that she would make reservations at McDonald's, if possible.

"This early in the season, we have tables available. A couple weeks from now, it becomes more difficult." The woman took two menus from behind the hostess station, leading the two friends to a table by a window, where the early summer sun still cast its warm, welcoming light.

Annie opened her menu. "Did you get some rest this afternoon?"

"After coming back from shopping and having a snack, I stretched out for what I thought was going to be a short nap," Seneca began. "Next thing I knew it was five thirty! You should have seen me hopping around, trying not to be late."

"You weren't kidding when you said you needed some relaxation, were you?"

Seneca glanced over the top of her menu. "It was probably from all the driving."

Annie lowered her own menu to gape at her friend. "You drove? That's an odd way to relax, Seneca. I've made the same drive, and it's a monster. Why didn't you fly?"

Seneca looked around, as if trying to locate the waitress. "I've come to associate flying with work—flying to interviews or conferences. I just had a hankering to take my time, for once."

"I can understand that," said Annie. And she did, but she couldn't shake the perception beginning to invade her thoughts—the one whispering to her that her friend of so many years was hiding something. Something important.

~ 3 ~

Annie lowered her eyes once again to her menu and asked in what she hoped was a casual tone, "How are Hunter and the kids doing?"

"They're all well," Seneca began. "Hunt always enjoys those first couple of quiet weeks during summer break. Says he gets more accomplished then than between August and May." Her husband had been the principal at Brookfield High for over a decade, but summer vacation was far from a vacation for a school administrator. "Jake's doing well at his company and starts his MBA in the fall." She shook her head as she mused, "I never would have thought he'd turn out to be such a business-minded person after his rambunctious childhood. The sight of him sitting behind a desk still confuses me, but I'm so proud of him."

Annie chuckled. "I still remember LeeAnn trying to get him to play school with her, she as the teacher, of course. I guess it never occurred to her seven-year-old mind that she'd actually have to sit on him to get Jake to stay put!"

Shoulders shaking from her amusement, Seneca said, "Oh, I could have warned LeeAnn, if I'd been there!"

The conversation paused as their waitress came to take their order. Once their ice teas had been served, Annie asked, "And what's Jessie up to now?"

Seneca tore the top off a packet of stevia and poured it

into her glass. "She's spending the summer in Italy, studying art history and toying with the idea of changing her major to international relations."

"Wow! How exciting! How's Mama handling her adventure?" With her own parents having been world travelers, Annie had braced herself for the possibility of LeeAnn wanting to explore faraway places, but her daughter had generally stuck close to home. Annie had to admit to herself, she'd been relieved.

"I'm mostly proud of her for delving into possibilities," Seneca replied. "Although my heart relocated into my throat several times while we were packing and seeing her off at the airport."

"I hear you!" Annie sympathized. Noticing a blond woman with oversized glasses she'd recognize anywhere heading toward their table, Annie waved. "Hi, Valerie! Come meet my friend from Texas."

When the fifty-something woman arrived beside their table, Annie made introductions. "Seneca, Valerie has been a great help to me—she's very patient when I hound her for information at the library."

The cornflower blue eyes behind the reference librarian's glasses sparkled. "Don't let Annie fool you. We all love helping her with her mysteries, no hounding necessary."

"I have a deep respect for librarians," said Seneca. "One of the major reasons I'm in my profession is because of the love of reading and then writing that was sparked at my childhood public library."

The natural curiosity that had led the librarian to her

own profession was immediately revealed. "Wonderful! What's your career?"

"I'm a reporter for a Texas newspaper—the same paper at which I started as an intern way too many years ago!" Seneca fidgeted with her long teaspoon.

A look of excitement came across the librarian's face. "I have an idea! We've been putting together a summer series about different careers for the town's youth—one-hour presentations, including a question-and-answer time. Seneca, would you be interested in kicking the series off?"

The teaspoon continued to weave through the reporter's fingers as she considered the idea. "Well, I might be able to do it."

"I know you're on vacation, Seneca, but you can do that sort of presentation in your sleep by now," Annie said.

Valerie rushed to add, "We'd love to have you, and we'll advertise about you and your topic on our website and in other media to make sure we have a good crowd so it'll be worth your time."

The teaspoon slipped through Seneca's fingers, clattering onto the table. "Y'all know how to plan a successful series, for sure." Her eyes dropped away from the librarian's face as she rested her hand over the wayward spoon. "As much as I'd like to help, I promised my husband I'd actually rest for my entire vacation. As Annie can tell you, I tend toward being a workaholic."

Annie nodded solemnly. "She doesn't just tend; her friends have nagged her for years about slowing down to smell the roses more. I wouldn't want Hunt to be mad at me for tempting you to break your word to him."

Seneca finally raised remorseful eyes to the librarian. "I'm so sorry."

The woman waved aside the apology. "Please don't give it another thought. I understand completely. My own husband is giving me the eye as I speak, so I'd better get back to our table. Enjoy your dinner and your visit!"

Seneca's eyes followed the librarian as she made her way across the dining room, and Annie peeked at her friend while her eyes were elsewhere. Annie had never before heard her friend turn down the chance to talk about journalism and that—plus Seneca's obvious nervousness about the publicity—only added to her sense of something weighing on her friend. The attention of both women was redirected when their salads arrived.

"I'm glad I decided to come to Stony Point for my vacation, Annie." Seneca dipped her salad fork into the petite cup of creamy dressing nestled against the side of the salad bowl and speared a cherry tomato half. "As much as you hear folks talk about the cool manners of Yankees, I haven't seen it here in Stony Point."

Annie wondered if Seneca was trying to divert her attention from the refusal to speak at the library and then chided herself for being overly suspicious. "I won't lie and say there wasn't a period of adjustment when I first arrived in town, when some people didn't trust me because I wasn't from the region. I don't know if the fact that my grandparents were beloved residents for so many years made it easier on me, but I've grown to love the people of Stony Point, quirks and all." Annie folded a large lettuce leaf before piercing it with her fork.

"I can tell from your letters. When I see one in the mailbox, I know there'll be a good story or two to enjoy." Seneca paused. "Do you think the proximity of most of the residents helps in keeping the friendly vibe of the town? You know how it is back home. Some families are miles from their next-door neighbors. It's too easy to be isolated, I think."

Annie sat back in her chair, considering Seneca's point. "I would have to agree. I found it entirely too easy to isolate myself after Wayne's death. If I hadn't had so many dear friends, I could have stayed a recluse for years. When I arrived here, I only knew one person, Alice, and she was none too pleased with how I had dropped our correspondence when I started college." Annie thought back to the day she had seen her childhood friend walking up the driveway of Grey Gables, a chilly expression on her face. "How blessed I've been that she forgave my foolishness. She worked hard to make it easier for me to be woven into the fabric of the community."

The waitress brought their main course, Gulf of Maine red fish for Annie and lobster carbonara for Seneca.

"I like your fabric analogy," Seneca said after the waitress had assured herself that the two diners had everything they needed. "Still crocheting up a storm?" She hovered her fork over the mound of pasta covered with succulent shellfish before nipping a few strands of angel hair pasta and twirling it on her fork.

Annie cut off a square of a wide ribbon of zucchini. "Of course," answered Annie. "The Hook and Needle Club has been active in Stony Point for decades, and it has definitely encouraged me to try a myriad of different designs. Last year we even made chicken sweaters for a local animal shelter!"

"Chicken sweaters?" Seneca raised an eyebrow. "Sweaters with chicken designs? Are they the state bird or something?" she joked.

Annie quickly raised her hand to clap it over her mouth, as she tried not to laugh before swallowing her food. "No! We actually knit or crocheted sweaters to be worn by chickens. The poultry had lost most of their feathers through neglect. The rescued chickens were taken to a shelter, and the director asked us to make the sweaters until the poor things grew their feathers back."

"Well, that makes a lot more sense." Seneca chuckled. "Now that I think about it, it reminds me of those penguins caught in an oil spill off the coast of New Zealand a few years ago. People knit sweaters for the penguins so they wouldn't ingest oil when they preened themselves. The photos were so adorable."

Annie set down her tea glass. "Exactly. Same concept. It certainly was a change of pace from shawls and booties."

"Did you make your sweater?" Seneca asked, eyeing the delicate leaf pattern covering her friend's arms. "It's beautiful."

Annie nodded, running a hand over the softness. "There's plenty of time for handwork over the frigid winter." She paused. "How would you like me to teach you to crochet while you're here? It's a perfect way to relax while still feeling like you're accomplishing something."

"Are you suggesting I have problems with relaxing?" Seneca sounded only half in jest.

As she thought over the many years she had known her friend, with her chaotic career and life, Annie didn't have to hesitate. "I most certainly am. If Hunt is having to insist you not work over your vacation, it only proves I'm right."

Seneca leveled her gaze at her friend. "Annie Dawson, you're getting too smart." She raised both her hands like a captured criminal. "I surrender. Bring on the crochet."

"You won't regret it," declared Annie. "We'll start tomorrow after lunch, and on Monday, we'll go to A Stitch in Time and buy you your own set of hooks and supplies."

Seneca smiled her agreement as she twirled another length of angel hair, snagging a tender piece of lobster before lifting the fork. "On one condition."

"What?"

"That you and I make sure we also spend a good deal of time walking." Seneca flourished her food-laden utensil. "This is the most delicious food I've had in ages, and I bet it has a gazillion calories. I'm not going to burn off enough just crocheting." As her mouth closed around the forkful, her eyes closed, and a look of bliss came over her face.

Annie grinned easily. "Deal. The lobster carbonara is worth every calorie, though. Ian says he's sure it will be served in heaven."

Seneca considered her friend as she raised her napkin to dab at the corner of her mouth. "And who is this Ian with the refined culinary taste?"

Annie hadn't realized she'd never told her friend about Ian Butler. "He's the mayor of Stony Point. Did you notice the lighthouse?" Seneca nodded. "It's named for his family; they were one of the earliest families to settle here."

"Ah." Seneca peered at Annie, cocking her head to the side and noticing the beginning of a blush. "Tell me more."

As her friend began to describe the man she'd come to love, and all the pangs and concerns that came with those deepening emotions, Seneca silently rejoiced. She'd been concerned that Annie's deep sense of loyalty to her deceased husband would keep her from ever considering a new relationship.

"Will I be able to meet Ian? He sounds like a man Wayne would have liked."

Annie pushed the remains of her meal around the plate. "I've thought that too," she said, growing contemplative.

Seneca recognized Annie's change of mood and reached over to grab her friend's hand. "So ... do I have to ask twice?" she said. "When do I meet Ian? Just so you don't forget."

The tense knot in her stomach had loosened. Relieved that her friend understood, Annie answered, "If you come to church with me tomorrow, you can meet Ian there, and I'm sure he'll want to spend some time getting to know you. He knows how important my friends from home are to me."

"I'd love to come with you to church. What time does the service start?"

Annie noticed the server was heading their way so she answered quickly. "I'll pick you up at ten thirty."

"Are you enjoying your meals?" The server again interrupted their planning.

Seneca sighed. "I drove all the way from Texas, and it was worth every mile for the lobster carbonara."

"Our chef will be happy to hear it." The server smiled. "Can I bring you some dessert?"

Annie answered. "None for me tonight, but the meal was delicious."

"Nothing for me, either." As Annie had suspected,

her friend still preferred to eat her sweet treats separate from meals.

When the server left, Annie told Seneca, "We need to go into Portland before you leave. There's a chocolate shop I've found where you must pick up a 'Maine mix' for your evening treat."

"Haven't forgotten my tradition, I see. Let's not wait too long before we go to Portland, then. I pretty much depleted my stash on the drive up," Seneca confessed. "What's in a Maine mix?"

Annie shook a finger at her friend. "Oh, no. It's a surprise, but I promise you'll love it." Her earlier concerns about the reasons for her friend's trip were forgotten. "I'm so happy you've come, Seneca!"

"I am too." A quick glance at Annie's footwear told her what she needed to know. "Now, as soon as the check comes, let's go walk in the gorgeous Maine summer air."

4

"Annie, what a charming church!" Seneca exclaimed as Annie pulled into the parking lot next to Stony Point Community Church. "It must be over a hundred years old."

Annie parked and then took the key from the ignition. "It is. It's not the original one, though. Stony Point, like many old towns, suffered a good deal of loss of property from fire. Compared to some buildings around Maine, this church is a youngster."

The two women walked toward the main front doors of the church. Annie pointed to the far right side of the building. "Over there is where Alice and I were sweating through Pilates yesterday morning before we saw you."

"I like churches that aren't empty shells six days of the week," said Seneca.

"The folks here take the 'community' part of the church's name seriously," Annie said. "Between the church and the Hook and Needle Club, there's no way I could be lonely, unless I was determined to be."

"It must be a big relief for LeeAnn to know you have such a strong support system here. I know she was worried at first when you decided to stay here." A stiff gust of breeze grabbed at the turquoise blazer Seneca wore over her sleeveless dress.

Annie would not soon forget the discussions she had had with her daughter while LeeAnn wrangled to discover the true desire of her mother's heart regarding the next step for her life. "I'm thankful LeeAnn had people like you to talk to. Seems she's made her peace with it now."

"Honestly, I think, deep down, she is proud of you," said Seneca, "for not doing the expected."

Taps of hurrying heels approached behind them. They turned to see Alice rushing to catch up. "I thought you Southerners were supposed to be slow walkers!" she chuffed.

"Talk fast, walk fast is what I learned from thirty years in the newspaper business," Seneca explained. "But since I'm on vacation now, I'll try to revert back to Dixie speed. How did your party go last night?"

"Could have been better; could have been worse. Dinner with you two would have been much more fun."

Sending her best friend a consoling look, Annie reached out to open the door into the vestibule of the church. "We'll just have to make sure we entertain you twice as much this afternoon."

Alice dropped her voice as she stepped over the threshold. "I can deal with that. Hey, are you feeling sore today?" She nodded thanks to the usher who handed her a bulletin.

Waiting until she had moved past the usher, Annie whispered her answer. "Not too much, except my core. Obviously, I've not kept my girlish waist as well as I thought I had."

Alice chuckled, gesturing up the aisle to where Ian Butler stood, watching their approach. "From the way our mayor's looking at you right now, I'm thinking it doesn't matter much."

With her powers of observation built over decades of reporting, Seneca seemed to take in a full picture of Annie's love interest without appearing to even notice his existence. She turned to Annie, murmuring, "Quite a handsome catch, my friend."

"He could still slip the hook," Annie said. Then, to keep the mood light, she added, "Or I might want to throw him back, you know."

Seneca's eyes flickered between Annie and the man. "He's looking pretty happy on that hook to me. I think it's been too long since you've seen him with fresh eyes—the kind of eyes I happen to have."

"Could we just focus on the worship service, please?" Annie pleaded, as they continued up the aisle closer to Ian.

When they were a few steps away, Ian approached the three women and addressed Seneca. "Welcome to Stony Point. I'm Ian Butler." He extended his right hand to her.

"It's a pleasure to meet you, Mayor Butler." Seneca's voice lilted into her Southern belle cadence as she shook his hand. "I'm an old friend of Annie's."

The edges of Ian's brown eyes crinkled with his widening smile. "So I've heard from Mike Magruder. We always enjoy meeting Annie's family and friends from Texas." He nodded to Alice and kissed Annie lightly on the cheek, pulling them into the conversation. "I've been plotting with my brother, Todd, and we're having a lobster bake after church. I hope you all will be able to join us."

Alice's hands went to her hips, arms akimbo. "Now Ian, how did you know I made a double batch of rhubarb cobbler yesterday?"

"I had no idea, Alice. Let's chalk it up to delicious providence, if you're willing to share." Ian glanced over his shoulder when the prelude music ended, seeing Reverend Wallace standing to approach the front. He escorted the ladies to a pew. "After the service, I'll give you the details." He stood back as the trio filed into the row and then settled himself next to the aisle.

For the next hour, Annie kept her focus trained on the service, enjoying having Seneca beside her. They had not attended the same church in Brookfield. Her friend's beautiful alto voice surprised Annie, and she realized she had never heard Seneca sing. Seneca's smooth harmony made it obvious how often she had sung the hymns. Annie hoped the music and message would help soothe whatever it was that seemed to be throwing her friend off kilter.

After the service, Annie introduced Seneca to the many friends who came to greet her. Todd Butler joined Ian on the outskirts of the group, apparently finalizing plans for the lobster bake. Annie caught the lobsterman's eye and waved, expecting him to come closer to be introduced. But the powerfully built man simply nodded in response, clapped his taller brother on the shoulder, and strode for a side exit.

While Peggy was chatting with Seneca, with her husband Wally standing shyly beside her, Annie slipped over to Ian. "Is Todd all right? Is the lobster bake still on for lunch? I'd be happy to host everyone at Grey Gables, if needed."

Ian rested an arm across her shoulder. "That's thoughtful of you, Annie, but it won't be necessary." He leaned down and spoke softly. "The bake is still on schedule, but Todd's lobster shack was broken into last night."

"Oh, no!" Annie gasped in dismay. "Was there much taken?"

"Strangely, no," Ian answered. "Not a rope, buoy, net, pot, or trap gone. I'm wondering if someone just needed a place to sleep for the night."

Annie's concentration drew a slight frown on her usually cheerful face. "You don't suppose it could have been Breck, do you? I know his home life isn't pleasant." The lanky teen with an unruly mane of tawny hair who worked at The Cup & Saucer had crept into Annie's heart as he tried so hard and quietly to overcome a hard beginning in life. How she hoped he wasn't the one who had broken into Todd's shack.

Ian's arm tightened around Annie, drawing her closer. "I don't think it was Breck. Both Jeff and Marie have given him open invitations to stay at their homes, if he needs to. Can't think why he'd go to a shack when he can be much more comfortable elsewhere."

Although Ian would never admit it, Annie had the suspicion that those invitations from Jeff, the owner of The Cup & Saucer, and Marie, who was the cook there, were the brainchild of the man next to her. The man was a public servant through every cell of his body, caring deeply for all of Stony Point's citizens.

"I hope you're right. Is there anything we can do to help? Did the intruder leave a mess?" Having had her house invaded and ransacked more than once, Annie had become an expert on quick cleanups.

Again Ian answered, "No. Everything was left in its place. That's why I'm thinking someone simply needed a place to stay. Todd just needs to go file a report of the break-in with the police. Then, he'll meet us and Becky on the beach for the bake." Annie was glad to hear Todd's wife would be joining them, as she didn't often have the chance to talk with Becky. "Come to the North Beach after you've gotten comfortable."

With a final warm hug, Ian released Annie and moved through the lingering crowd, heading for the door where Reverend Wallace stood. Alice approached with Seneca following. "So what's the plan?" she asked.

"The plan is to go change into comfortable clothes and then meet Ian and the others at the North Beach." Most of the coastline bordering Stony Point was rugged, fun for climbing but not necessarily for lobster bakes. The North Beach area was sandy and much more conducive to picnicking, especially at low tide. "Alice, why don't you ride with us?"

"I should drive, Annie," Alice said. "You might want to do something with Seneca after the picnic, and I have some things I need to do at the house later."

"OK." Annie turned to Seneca. "Now promise me you won't lay down for a quick rest and sleep through the bake."

Still in the sanctuary, Seneca kept her laugh soft. "No fear, Annie. I slept extremely well last night. No napping needed ... at least until after lunch."

"Good! I'll drop you off, and then I'll pick you back up after Alice and I have changed," Annie told her as the three women approached Reverend Wallace at the door. "Good morning, Reverend. I'd like you to meet my friend Seneca Marchal. She's visiting from my hometown in Texas."

His eyes merry behind his glasses, the minister grasped Seneca's hand in both of his. "It's a pleasure to meet you, Seneca. I hope you're enjoying your time in Maine."

"Thank you, Reverend Wallace," said Seneca. "Annie has landed in a beautiful place. Don't be surprised if I find other excuses to come visit her more often after experiencing the charm of Stony Point."

The minister released her hand to grasp Annie's. "No excuses necessary—just come!"

Annie looked over her shoulder at her friend as she squeezed Reverend Wallace's hand. "Now you have to come back, Seneca. How about in winter? Hunt can learn how to ski on something besides water," she said.

"That's not a bad idea," Seneca agreed. "But who's going to teach him?"

Reverend Wallace moved his handshake from Annie to Alice. "Rest assured it won't be me! I'm much more suited to eating my wife's pie by the fire than skiing these days." He glanced down for a moment at the generous girth of his middle. "Obviously."

After dropping Seneca off at the inn and returning to Grey Gables, Annie quickly changed clothes and gathered everything she needed for an afternoon at the beach, her cat, Boots, watching her every move. Annie had inherited Boots along with Grey Gables after the death of her grandmother. When she walked back to the kitchen and paused in front of the refrigerator, her white-footed companion rubbed against her ankle. Absentmindedly, Annie bent to stroke the soft smoky-gray fur behind Boots's ears, murmuring as the cat closed her eyes and pressed her head against Annie's hand. "I've been gone a lot this weekend, haven't I? After the lobster bake, I promise to bring a friend to visit you. Would you like that?"

The feline housemate cocked her head, as if considering

the news of a visitor and opened her eyes. Annie chuckled. "You'll like Seneca, Boots. She loves animals. Well, except snakes." After one last caress, Annie straightened and went back to considering what to bring to the lobster bake. She'd made a large summer salad for lunching with Seneca and Alice, and she thought it was large enough to share with the rest of the group. Was there anything else?

Early Saturday morning, Annie had perused the local farmers market, thrilled to find just-picked asparagus. It was something she had not yet added to her garden plot, so Annie had snatched up a large quantity, planning to prepare some for freezing. Instead, she would bring it all to the lobster bake for grilling.

After washing her hands, Annie settled a large colander in the deep farmhouse-style sink and retrieved the bundle of asparagus from the refrigerator. After trimming off the tough ends and gently rinsing the stalks, Annie moved the dark green asparagus to a large oblong dish before drizzling them with olive oil and sprinkling them with some sea salt. *All set for grilling,* Annie thought, as she covered the dish with foil. She was retrieving the large salad bowl from the refrigerator when Alice knocked at the back door with her elbow, two long dishes of cobbler in her hands.

"Perfect timing," Annie told her friend after opening the door. "Everything's ready to go."

"Watch out for the cooler on the steps," Alice warned. "I couldn't bring cobbler without the vanilla ice cream, you know."

Annie surveyed the items she was taking, deciding what to load first. "Let's take the cooler out to the trunk first."

Alice set the cobblers on the oak table while Annie grabbed her keys. Soon the car was loaded, and they were on their way to pick up Seneca. When they pulled up to the curb in front of the main entrance of the inn, Seneca was already waiting, comfortable in denim capris and a sunny yellow cotton shirt with a hobo bag slung over one shoulder.

"You look cheerful," Alice told Seneca as she slid onto the seat behind her. "I couldn't wear that shade of yellow for love or money, but it's gorgeous on you."

Seneca secured her seatbelt. "Staying away from yellow is a small price to pay for your beautiful hair color, though. I look abysmal in most neutrals." She looked over at Annie's dishes resting on the other side of the seat. "I feel like I should be bringing something to contribute. Maybe we should stop at Magruder's on our way?"

"Don't think another second about it," said Annie. "Ian would be appalled if you brought anything. Just relax and enjoy."

Seneca's mouth opened, as if she thought to argue the point, but decided against it. "All right, if you insist. I'll let y'all feed me with no fuss. I'm almost giddy at the thought of an afternoon on the beach. It's been so long since I've taken a beach trip." She stared out the window as they drove along Ocean Drive.

"I never get tired of it," said Annie, "and thanks to Grandpa's foresight to buy all the acreage between Grey Gables and the shoreline, I'm blessed to enjoy the ocean any day I want to."

"And thanks to my foresight to make Annie a friend, I get to enjoy it too." Alice grinned. "Make sure you get some great photos of the surf to take back to Texas with you—and maybe some sea glass."

Annie pulled off the road, moving slowly forward until she was positioned safely out of traffic. The three women piled out of the car and pulled the bounty from the trunk and backseat. Alice sheltered her eyes with a hand and peered along the beach until she saw the long portable table and the other necessities for a lobster bake. "It's this way." She led the way through a break in the rocks, the sand tamped down by a steady stream of visitors.

Ian was bent over a giant lobster pot perched over the frame of a gas-fueled portable burner. The short sleeves of his sport shirt revealed the tan forearms of a man who spent plenty of time outdoors, in spite of his long hours of work at Town Hall. As the three women drew close, he settled the lid over the pot and straightened to his full height. "Looks like you ladies have brought more than Alice's cobbler."

"Is there room on the grill for some farm-fresh asparagus?" Annie asked, flourishing her foil-covered dish.

Ian turned to his right and yelled over the sounds of the ocean. "Hey, Todd! Make some room on the grill. Annie's brought asparagus."

Ian's younger brother nodded, picking up a pair of long tongs to shift pieces of chicken.

Seneca held the large salad but stood taking deep gulps of ocean air and gazing at the water. "Mmm, there's no perfume like this in any department store."

Annie glanced at her friend, hoping the calming balm of the sea would soothe Seneca and give her respite from whatever seemed to be haunting her.

~5~

Seneca's sea trance also caught Ian's attention. "Looks like your friend is lost in space and time," he said softly to Annie. In his normal take-charge voice he announced to all three of the women, "Becky's in charge of the drinks and other food items. She'll take care of whatever's in that big bowl." He gestured at a small dingy a few feet from the table, listing at a jaunty angle against a rock. "How do you like our drink station?"

Puzzled, Annie stepped closer for a better look. "I love it. What a clever idea!" The dingy was filled with ice, and bottles and cans of sodas, teas, and sparkling water. "Your sister-in-law would make a wonderful party planner."

"What's Moxie?" Seneca came up beside her, having switched her gaze from the ocean to the beverage boat, noticing a red can festooned with the name. "I've never heard of it."

Ian reached into the dingy for one of the red cans and held it out to Seneca. "Moxie was created by a man who was born in Union, Maine, so it's a regional favorite. It's been around since the eighteen hundreds. You can't go home to Texas without trying one."

"As Annie knows, I'll taste just about anything once." Seneca turned to her friend and handed her the salad bowl, and then took the can from Ian. "Should I try this now or with lunch?"

Annie hesitated, not wanting to admit she found the drink unappetizing.

Ian came to her rescue. "I'd suggest trying a sample in a cup first. If you don't like it, someone else will finish the can for you. The cups are over by the condiments. To my taste buds, Moxie is the perfect accompaniment for red snappers."

"I'll get a cup for you, Seneca." Annie strode over to the table to deposit the salad among the other side dishes and lifted a cup from the stack next to a basket filled with sturdy plastic dinnerware.

"Red snappers?" Seneca raised an eyebrow at Ian. "You mean like the fish?"

"In this case red snappers are hot dogs with dyed-red casings," Ian explained.

"I don't think we have those in Texas either. How am I going to decide between all these tempting food options?"

Ian grinned. "No decision needed; taste them all."

"I'm not sure that would count as 'moderation in all things,' which is usually my motto," Seneca replied. "Though I suppose vacations weren't created for moderation anyway."

"No, they weren't, yet they provide an important balance in our lives, don't they?" Ian glanced at his watch. "Please excuse me, I need to check the lobsters. Wouldn't want to ruin your first authentic Maine lobster bake with tough crustaceans."

"Absolutely not." Seneca's eyes followed the mayor as he returned to the stainless steel pot, a smile starting to bloom from the corners of her mouth.

Annie reappeared and held a lime green cup out to her. "What has you smiling?"

"I like him, your mayor." Seneca turned her gaze from Ian to her friend.

Alice approached in time to hear Seneca's comment. "I haven't met many females who don't like Ian. He really is one of a kind. But he only has eyes for our Annie."

Annie gave a shy smile. "Maybe."

"Maybe nothing," Alice declared, always one to call things as she saw them.

Todd, accustomed to speaking over the roar of wind and surf, yelled from his station at the grill. "Hey, you three! If you want your food hot, you better come fast!"

"You don't have to call us twice!" Alice hollered back. "Come on, girls."

"'Time'a eat,' as John used to say," Annie added, laughing at the memory of her grandson when he was a toddler. The women hurried to the table to pick up plates, Seneca placing her soda can and cup beside a place setting. Seeing Todd's wife standing nearby, Annie smiled at her. "Becky, you've made everything look so inviting, please go get your food while it's hot."

"Thank you, Annie. I'll do that as soon as I track down Patrick and Sarah." The middle-aged woman's brown eyes scanned the shoreline under arched brows. "They've wandered into the rocks with Tartan, I think."

Alice wouldn't hear of it. "I'll go tell them. I can shout almost as loud as Todd. Go on and grab your food."

Becky tucked a stray lock of blond hair behind her ears and wiped her hands on a damp cloth she carried in her apron pocket. "I appreciate that, Alice. Don't feel like you have to escort them once you find them. Just let them know the food's ready and come get your lunch."

"Gotcha." Alice headed one way to find the youngsters and Becky, Annie, and Seneca the other.

Annie introduced Seneca to Becky as they walked over the sand, keeping a firm grip on their plates to keep the sturdy ocean breeze from turning them into Frisbees. More loquacious than her husband, yet still reserved, Becky quietly welcomed Seneca to Stony Point.

"Have you lived here all your life?" The reporter couldn't hold back her instinctive curiosity.

Becky's eyes followed the path of a gull until she had ascertained it wasn't heading for the table of food left unattended. "Yes, I was born here. My parents moved from the Boston area, though, when they were newlyweds. Todd and Ian's parents were the first people to befriend them." Approaching the grill, she surveyed the contents. "The asparagus looks perfect. Where did you get it?"

"The Van Syckel booth at the farmers market," Annie answered. "I'd buy everything from them, if I didn't grow most of my own. I told them they must be kindred spirits with Gram. They have the same way with produce that she did. Turns out they knew both Gram and Grandpa."

Becky nodded as she held out her plate to receive the asparagus Todd was scooping off the grill with tongs. "The same thing happens to me, except it's people who know the Butlers. When Patrick was in elementary school, his classmates called me the lighthouse lady, even though I had simply married into the family." Murmuring her thanks to her husband, she stepped aside to make room for Seneca and Annie at the grill.

After the women had selected their grilled items, they

moved over to the lobster pot, where Ian stood clacking his metal tongs. Seneca peeked over the edge of the pot at the banded lobsters and informed the cook, "Last night I had lobster carbonara at Maplehurst Inn. You have a hard act to follow, Ian."

"I certainly do!" Ian admitted. "I've eaten many a meal at the inn, and it's hard to beat that particular dish. But there's something to be said for simplicity, as well. Just a little melted butter for dipping one of these bad boys, and you'll be truly experiencing a Maine phenomenon." After considering the pile of crustaceans, he selected one and settled it onto Seneca's plate. "Don't forget to grab a bib."

Seneca stared down at the lobster nestled next to the asparagus, its tough shell a bright red. "Um, who's going to help me figure out how to eat this thing?"

"It had better be someone other than me," admitted Annie. "I still haven't gotten the hang of it yet, so I'll just stick to teaching you to crochet. I can tell you that Ian's right about using a bib. Your shirt's too pretty to be ruined with lobster juice."

"The rest of us will show you enough technique to get you fed," Ian assured Seneca before she headed back to the table.

"Chef's choice for mine," Annie told Ian, holding out her plate. Leaning closer as he considered the remaining creatures, she continued, "Thank you for putting this together so fast. It's such a thoughtful way to welcome Seneca."

"You're welcome." Ian shifted one lobster to reach the one underneath it, and then tonged the lower one to examine it. Satisfied, he presented it to Annie. "How about this one?"

"You know I always ask the butcher to select my meat," said Annie. "I'll trust you to give me a tasty lobster." Bracing her plate with one hand, fingers splayed for support, she placed her free hand on Ian's forearm and gave a gentle squeeze. She tiptoed up, found his lips and kissed him gently. "Thank you again."

Warmth from a source other than the steaming pot in front of him rose in Ian's eyes. "It's my pleasure, Annie."

"I'll save you a seat," Annie murmured and returned to the long table to sit next to Seneca, one chair free on her other side. Seneca had already donned a bib from the collection displayed in an antique tin pail in the middle of the table. Annie availed herself of one as well and tied it with a flourish.

Alice returned from the rocks with teenaged Patrick, his little sister, Sarah, and Ian's schnauzer, Tartan. She filled her plate with the enticing food and sat next to Seneca. Holding her own lobster by its back, she demonstrated to Seneca how to twist and break off the legs and then its claws. The corner of her bottom lip clasped between her teeth, Seneca mirrored Alice's movements, waving a claw in triumph when it snapped off at the first joint. "Got it!"

"Now remove the loose part of the claw. And don't forget to dig out the morsel in there; it's very tasty," Alice cautioned.

Tapping the large crusher claw with a fingernail, Seneca asked, "How do I get this open?"

Alice flourished a nutcracker from a pile of them in the center of the table. "That's where these come in handy." Holding the wider end of the claw, Alice broke off the tip with the cracker. Then she set the cracker on the plastic-covered table and pushed the meat from the tip of the claw out the larger side with a forefinger. Dipping the tender meat in the ramekin of melted butter on her plate, Alice took a bite.

Following Alice's lead, Seneca opened the large claw on her own plate and drew out the white meat. Her eyes closed as the buttery morsel practically melted in her mouth. "Oh, Ian's so right. There *is* something to be said for simplicity, and that something is sublime!"

"When you've dug out all the tasty claw morsels, I'll show you what to do with my personal favorite, the tail," offered Becky, sitting across from Seneca.

Todd nudged his wife's arm. "Will you show her how to eat the tomalley?"

Betsy leveled a no-nonsense gaze at him. "I don't think so."

"Do I want to know what the tomalley is?" Seneca asked tentatively. "Something tells me you're not talking about the traditional Mexican pork dish."

Annie covered her mouth to keep from spitting out a tidbit of lobster and then swallowed carefully. "Probably not while you're still eating. It's definitely not anything like t-a-m-a-l-e-s."

"Hard-core lobster lovers eat the tomalley, but suffice it to say it's probably not the healthiest thing to consume," inserted Ian, "without giving enough detail to ruin your appetite."

Seneca's eyes passed between Ian and Annie's faces. "I'll take your word on it and pass on that particular part of the lobster. So Alice, don't let me stumble on it by accident, OK?"

"You got it," Alice promised. "I've been known to play

practical jokes now and then, but feeding you tomalley won't be one of them."

Popping a tiny morsel from a small section of a claw into her mouth, Seneca's eyes went to her unopened soda can. "I'm not going to pass on the Moxie, however." After carefully draining the water from the melted ice out of the cup, she poured some of the dark liquid over the remaining cubes. Raising the cup, she declared, "Here's to old friends, new friends, and new experiences!"

The others at the table joined in her toast, keeping their attention on her reaction to the Moxie. She sipped, paused, and sipped some more before sharing her opinion. "It's different; not like those knockoffs of mainstream sodas. Not as sweet, either. I think it'll grow on me."

"We'll make sure you have a six-pack to take back to Texas," said Alice, a ring of approval in her voice. "I can't get Annie to like it, and I've been trying since we were kids!"

Annie chuckled. "I'm not sure why it's so important to Alice for me to like that drink. You'd think she had a lot of stock in the company or something."

"You've probably been drinking too much sweet tea to like it," Seneca pondered. "And you know I like really dark chocolate, which has a slight bitterness to it, as Moxie does."

Alice snapped her fingers. "I never noticed the connection! Annie doesn't really like the dark, dark chocolate, even though she tries to. So it's not surprising she's not a fan of Moxie."

"Personally, I think it's better to *have* moxie, than to drink it, and our Annie has plenty of it!" Everyone looked in the direction of the newcomer's voice. Peggy

Carson and her family had managed to approach through the sand so quietly the group had not heard them coming.

Ian stood. "Peggy, Wally, and Emily—you made it! There's still plenty of food so help yourselves."

"I'm sorry we're late, Mr. Mayor," said Peggy. "Em just got a new hedgehog, and we got carried away feeding and watching it."

The Carsons' daughter, Emily, was fast approaching her mother's height at the age of ten, and her energy rivaled Peggy's as well. "You should see it, Mr. Butler! It's the cutest thing ever! And Dad made it a two-room hedgie home."

Wally Carson was a handyman, and his building prowess was well known, but he ran a hand through his unruly hair thinking about his latest project. "Didn't expect it to take as long as it did, but the critter seems content now."

"Come on, Em," said Peggy. "Let's get our food before you tell everyone all about him."

Annie jumped up to provide the three newcomers with plates and dinnerware. Soon they were settled at the table, plates laden with food. In between bites of red snappers and the potato salad her mother had brought, Emily regaled everyone with her stories of their newest family member, on whose name they had not yet settled.

Glancing at Seneca, Annie expected to see a different kind of look on her friend's face. Seneca loved animals as much as she did, and knew James Herriot's books practically by heart. Yet, Seneca's eyes had an undertone of shadow as she listened intently to the young girl.

When everyone's plates were empty, except for lobster shells, Alice clapped her hands together. "Now, who's ready for rhubarb cobbler and ice cream?" The only immediate responses were groans.

"Will the ice cream keep on ice a while longer, Alice?" Annie asked. "I need some gentle exercise before I can fully enjoy your dessert."

Seneca nodded in agreement. "If y'all don't mind, I'd love to look for some sea glass to take home as a memento of my visit." She smiled at Annie. "The last time I saw LeeAnn and the twins, they amused me with their chatter about how many special pieces of glass they'd found."

"Em here is an expert sea glass hunter," Peggy informed her. "Would you like her to go with you?"

The young girl dashed over to slip her melamine plate into the large pan of water prepared for soaking. "I helped Joanna find some doozies. One was shaped just like a heart!"

"I'd like for you to come, Emily," said Seneca. "And anyone else who wants to." She followed Emily's example by clearing off the lobster shells and depositing her plate. "Are you coming, Becky?"

The woman glanced at her watch. "I'd like to, but the kids have plans for the rest of the day, and I need to drop them off. I'll try to be back in time for dessert, though."

Patrick and Sarah quickly cleared their places of any debris and bid the other picnickers farewell. "Thanks for lunch, Dad, Uncle Ian, and Annie." Patrick turned to his mother. "Mom, can you bring home some of Alice's cobbler for us?"

With a straight face their mother replied, "If there's any left." Then she waved to everyone and they made their way toward their SUV.

Those who remained waited while Ian and Todd made sure the cooking implements were safe to leave. Then the group spread out like an amiable net, flowing along the sand in search of sea glass.

~ 6 ~

The sun had dropped significantly lower in the sky by the time the glass hunters meandered back to their picnic area, pockets and hands bearing the results of their labor.

"Surely that was enough time and effort to make room for some cobbler, Annie." Both hands together, Seneca cupped her collection of amber, clear, green, and blue glass.

Annie padded over to the beach bag she had left tucked under the bench by the table. "I agree. I think I can force myself to eat a bit of Alice's cobbler now." She pulled out a couple of plastic storage bags, opening one for Seneca. "Here, for your glass." Holding the bag open, she waited until her friend had emptied her treasures into it and then zipped it shut. "If you'd like, I can take them home and give them a good cleaning along with mine. I promise I won't forget to give them to you before you leave."

"I'd appreciate that, Annie." Seneca tried to wipe her hands free of sand on her pants. "I doubt the housekeepers at Maplehurst Inn would appreciate my using their pristine white towels to clean ocean residue from the glass."

Alice reached into her bag for a pack of wipes, pulling out one for each of her friends, as well as herself. "Here, these work a little better than denim," she said, handing one to Seneca. "Who wants cobbler?" She looked at those around her.

"Isn't the question more like 'is there anyone who doesn't want cobbler?'" Ian said, chuckling. His schnauzer chose that moment to push his nose into the palm of his master's hands. "No, I'm not including you in the question, Tartan." The dog cocked his head to one side, as though not able to believe his ears.

Todd strode over to the cooled grill, eyeing a lone hot dog resting in the corner. "How about Tartan finishing up the last wiener?"

His brother ran his hand over the wiry hair of the dog's head and fondled an ear. "He did get a couple of nice runabouts. Sure, Todd, let him finish it off."

Lifting the red snapper, Todd dangled it. "Come here, boy!" Tartan's head perked up and every muscle in his body tensed as he looked first at the tempting morsel and then at Ian.

"Go get it, Tartan!" Ian nodded and then laughed with the others as Tartan sprang over to the grill, snatching the food in midair almost as soon as Todd tossed it his way.

Alice shook her head in mock seriousness. "Yes, it's truly a dog-eat-dog world." Making her way to the cooler to dig the ice cream out of the bed of ice she'd tucked it in, she asked, "Now, is there anyone who does not want cobbler or ice cream?" In the silence, while no one spoke up to decline the dessert, the faint buzz of a cellphone sounded. Both Ian and Todd instinctively glanced at the phones attached to their belts, and then both looked up again.

"Oh, it's mine." Alice handed the tub of ice cream to Annie and grabbed her phone, peering at the number. "That's odd. Angela doesn't usually call me on Sunday afternoon.

She's usually out with Mother." She unlocked the phone, walking away from her friends as she answered, "Hi, Angela. What's up?" After a pause she said, "You have? Why?" Her voice had turned serious.

Trying not to be nosy and listen in on the conversation, Annie took up the task of serving her friend's dessert. Seneca came beside her, and soon, delicious mounds of cobbler and ice cream graced a bowl for each person, including Alice. "Todd, we made a plate of cobbler for Becky and the kids, without the ice cream, of course. If she doesn't make it back in time, be sure to take it home with you."

"Thanks, Annie." Todd took his plate and scooped a hearty portion onto his fork. "Sometimes it takes a while for Becky to get away from the Smiths. Tina talks a boatload more than my wife does." Annie couldn't help but wonder how quiet the Todd Butler home was come evening when Todd was home from work, neither husband nor wife being big talkers. They were unassuming supporters of the Stony Point community, and she appreciated the strength of character they both possessed. She surely didn't mind, though, that Todd's brother enjoyed the art of conversation more than he did.

After a few minutes, during which most of the talk revolved around the way Alice had with rhubarb cobbler, the dessert-maker returned to the group gathered around the table. Annie opened her mouth to inform her friend how much everyone was enjoying her contribution when she saw how pale Alice's face had become. Quickly setting down her plate, she hurried to her side. "Are you OK?"

Alice shook her head and leaned against Annie,

all her usual energy drained from her voice when she answered. "Angela's been trying to reach me. I didn't hear it over all our noise." She took a deep breath, almost a gasp. "Mother's been rushed to the hospital. They think it might be a stroke." When Annie put her arms around her, Alice's head dropped against her shoulder. "Angela says it doesn't look good," she whispered. "I have to fly down there as soon as I can get a flight."

"Oh, Alice, I'm so sorry," Annie whispered back. "Let me help you get ready to go and drive you to the Jetport. Seneca can drive the Mustang home for you." She glanced over at her friend, who immediately nodded her agreement.

Concern written over his face, Ian approached while unhooking his phone from his belt. "Alice, would you like me to call the Jetport for the next available flight?"

"Thanks, Ian," Alice murmured. "I sure know how to close out a party, don't I?" Her friends took her attempt at humor in stride, knowing it had always been her way of dealing with stress.

Giving her distraught friend a quick hug, Annie began gathering their things together. Ian held his free hand over his left ear as he waiting for information from the airline customer-service call center at the Portland International Jetport. A minute later he reached into a pocket of his jeans for a small notepad and pen, positioning it on the lid of the now-cool grill to jot down the flight information. After thanking the customer-service representative, Ian disconnected and then tore the sheet from the pad.

Alice was facing the ocean, staring out past the curls of waves. Her eyes followed a sleek Northern Gannet as it soared on the air currents, but her mind was obviously much further south. Ian came alongside her, extending the sheet of paper to her. "You'll have to pack quickly. The flight leaves in four hours."

As she took the paper, Alice shifted her gaze to her long-time friend, who was talking with Seneca. "Thank you, Ian. Keep an eye on Annie while I'm gone, will you? I don't know how long I'll be away, and even with Seneca here, she could still stumble into trouble."

"You know I will." The man who could speak eloquently on most subjects at the drop of a hat hesitated, as if searching for the right words. "You know you and your family are in our prayers, Alice."

A quick nod was her only response as Annie and Seneca hurried up to them. "Everything's ready to go, Alice," Annie told her. "Did you get a flight?"

"Yes, my travel agent here found one in just four hours, so I'm glad you're planning to help me pack." Turning to Seneca, Alice said, "I'm sorry to disappear on you like this. I was looking forward to some more fun before you returned home." She pulled her car keys from a pocket, handing them to Seneca, who took them in one hand and warmly grasped her new friend's hand with the other.

"So was I, but maybe you'll be able to return before I leave," Seneca said hopefully.

"I hope so," Alice said, but there was doubt in her eyes. With that she followed Annie to her classic burgundy Chevrolet Malibu. Fastening her seat belt, she leaned against the headrest and closed her eyes while Annie backed out onto Ocean Drive. "I'm sorry to ruin your Sunday."

Annie would have given her one of those meaningful glances, but Alice's eyes were closed. "You hush up now, Alice MacFarlane," she said instead. "You haven't ruined a thing. I'm just relieved I'm here to help you so you can help your family."

Alice rubbed her right temple, fingers tracing a circular pattern. "I don't know how much they'll let me help." After a moment of silence, "Maybe if I had married a doctor like Mother wanted me to, I could do something of more significance. Really, what can I do? Angela has durable power of attorney, not me."

"There's a lot more to being supportive than signing legal papers," Annie reminded her. "You have a completely different personality than Angela, and that's good. You can offer your mother and even Angela a strength and perspective your sister doesn't have and never will. It's uniquely your own."

One side of Alice's mouth tilted up a smidgeon. "Careful, you're starting to sound like a sappy greeting card." She opened her eyes, settling her gaze on her friend. "But thanks. I'll try to remember what you said. I'm just scared."

"Of course you are. Who wouldn't be?" Annie spoke softly as she made sure the road was clear in both directions before maneuvering the car to back into the driveway of Alice's cottage. "There are few things as scary as having absolutely no control over the health of a loved one." How many times had she delved into that kind of fright? Her father, mother, grandparents, husband—all were taken from her as she had tried to hold on. It was like the earth's crust had splintered into minuscule fragments, leaving nothingness for a foothold. Then she was reminded of what God could do with nothing—He had created everything from nothing. So she wasn't going to admonish Alice to "look for the bright side," or assure her that her mother would quickly recover. "God is with you, Alice," she said quietly and simply.

"Thanks, Annie." Alice wiped the gathering tears with the back of her hand. "Feel free to send reminder texts every hour or so while I'm gone." She opened the car door. "We'd better hurry. At least packing should be simple. June in Florida doesn't exactly call for layers of clothing."

"Except in hospitals that tend to be freezing, even down South," Annie reminded her, as she followed Alice to the cottage's door. "So one or two long-sleeved sweaters or jackets would probably be helpful."

Alice stared at the locked door, motionless. "Uhh, I left my house key on the key ring I gave to Seneca."

"And it's for exactly those kinds of occurrences that you gave me a copy," Annie said, steering her friend around with a gentle arm toward Grey Gables. "Won't take but a moment."

"A brilliant bit of foresight, it was—us exchanging keys."

"One of my brightest friends came up with the idea," Annie said, as they climbed the steps to her wraparound porch. Inserting the key into her own front door, she asked over her shoulder, "Would you check Boots's water bowl while I grab the key?"

Her wan smile told Annie that Alice knew what she was doing, keeping her busy so she didn't dissolve into a puddle of anxiety. But she simply nodded and walked mechanically toward the kitchen, as Annie hurried into the living room to retrieve the spare door key from a drawer in the antique writing desk.

Key in hand, Annie entered the kitchen as Alice was carefully restoring the now full water bowl to its usual place on the floor. "Thanks! Let's go." As the two friends walked down the central hall, a gray blur appeared at the bottom of the staircase. Alice paused to bend down and caress the cat. "Sorry, Boots, I have to borrow Annie for a few more hours. But at least you have fresh water now." The cat opened its mouth, showing her teeth in a wide yawn, before padding toward the kitchen. "I appreciate your nonchalance about it."

"I guess Boots is finally beginning to get used to me being gone with the different road trips I've taken over the last year." Annie opened the front door and motioned her friend out ahead of her before exiting, pulling the door securely behind her. "I'm not sure if I should be relieved or insulted that I'm not special anymore."

A little smirk crossed Alice's lips. "Just wait; as soon as you think she doesn't care, Boots will pull something unexpected. That's exactly what she did after Betsy died."

"We'll see." Annie wasn't convinced. "She's a couple years older now, more mature."

"But still a cat." Alice plunged through the hedge.

Annie handed her the spare key as they approached the cottage. "Well, there is that."

In a matter of minutes after the two women disappeared into the cozy house, the car was packed with Alice's necessities, along with a bag of cross-stitch projects for the plane ride. Annie was thankful it was early in the summer—too early for the road south to Portland to be the typical parking lot it would morph into on Sunday afternoons once the true summer tourist season began. Instead, the traffic was manageable, and they arrived at the Jetport with plenty of time for Alice to purchase her ticket, go through security, and find her departure gate.

Annie stayed with her until her luggage was checked in and Alice was standing in line to go through security. "Keep me posted, if you have time, and call whenever you need to talk, no matter the time."

"Even if it's after 9 p.m.?" Alice quirked an eyebrow.

Annie nodded. "Even if. Try not to faint, it might look suspicious to security."

Alice surprised Annie by throwing her arms around her. "I don't know what I would have done, if you hadn't come back. Thank you."

"I don't know what I would have done, either," Annie answered back. "I really don't."

$$\sim 7 \sim$$

"How was Alice when you left her at the airport?" Seneca's concern registered in her voice through the phone.

Standing in front of the stove, waiting for the water for her evening herbal tea to boil, Annie thought of how her friend had embraced her with uncharacteristic emotion. "Emotional, for a person born and raised in Maine. But it encouraged me, actually. The last thing Alice needs to do is try to stiff-upper-lip this."

Briefly, Annie wondered if Seneca was trying to do the same with something in her life but decided it wasn't the time to ask. All she could do was to try to be as supportive and open with her Texan friend as possible, just like she had been with Alice. "I made sure she knew I wanted her to feel absolutely free to call me whenever she needed to talk, day or night. I hope she'll take me up on it." Annie also hoped Seneca would do the same.

There was a pause of silence before Seneca murmured, "So do I." Then her voice strengthened. "Hey, when did you want to pick out my crochet supplies? Tomorrow?"

"It depends. Do you have plans in the morning?" Annie supposed that after years of early rising for her hectic job, Seneca could be a chronic early riser like herself, but she didn't want to assume it.

"Nothing except to take another walk along the gorgeous shoreline again. Maybe look for some seals. I certainly don't see many of those around at home."

The kettle began to whistle softly, and then escalated to a high-pitched whine. "I know just the place for seal watching," Annie told her, removing the kettle from the burner and pouring water over the tea ball in her cup. "How would you like to have breakfast here at Grey Gables, and then we can make a day of shopping, walking, and seal watching? Followed by a crochet lesson, of course."

"Sounds like the perfect vacation day to me," Seneca answered. "What time should I come for breakfast, and should I bring anything?"

"Just your appetite."

"Well, if you haven't noticed yet, having an appetite has not been a problem since I arrived here." Seneca laughed. "Fitting into my clothes if I keep it up, however, may be!"

"I promise to make you a delicious but healthy breakfast," Annie promised her. "Is eight o'clock too early?"

Seneca gave a yip of a laugh. "Not at all. I'm usually up at five thirty most mornings at home, so an eight o'clock breakfast is downright decadent."

A yawn escaped, and Annie clapped her hand over her mouth to keep the sound from reaching Seneca's ears. Maybe the tea was unnecessary. It had been an unexpectedly busy Sunday. "Wonderful. Have a luxurious night's sleep."

"Thanks, Annie, it sounds like you will too." Annie could hear the smile in Seneca's voice. "Good night."

Annie wryly bid her friend the same and replaced the handset on the kitchen phone on the wall. Bringing the cup close to her lips, she gently blew on the hot liquid and enjoyed the aroma of the fragrant tea. She sat at the table, planning the healthy meal she had promised Seneca.

Once the tea was gone, and the menu complete, Annie took herself up the stairs, ready for that luxurious sleep. Boots had beaten her to it, curled in a loose ball with her tail covering her eyes in the middle of Annie's bed.

*　*　*　*

Early Monday morning found Annie in her garden, basking in the young day's sunshine as she banished weeds from her plants and selected some vegetables and herbs to use for breakfast. Ever since she had found her Gram's gardening journals, Annie had been expanding the variety of her planting. It seemed she learned something new every week of the growing season.

When she read her grandmother's notes about the use of zucchini blossoms, Annie tried them in her cooking and found the blossoms to be an interesting addition to her breakfast egg dishes. She hoped Seneca would enjoy them too. Annie perused the rows of zucchini plants, hunting for the thicker-stemmed blossoms, which indicated they were male. That way she could use the blossoms without having a negative impact on her zucchini harvest later in the summer.

Pinching off the blossoms was simultaneously relaxing and invigorating for Annie, as were most of the activities involved in gardening. What some people saw as a chore, Annie relished. It had been hard to find the time and motivation for gardening when she had lived in Texas and worked at the dealership most days. But now, Annie could pour the energy she had once used in her accounting work into other more physically active pursuits, and she was thankful for the change.

Annie considered the mound of zucchini blossoms in her harvest basket and decided she had gathered enough as she also planned to use spinach in the frittata she would make. As she moved on to the dark green leafy plants, Annie glanced over at Alice's cottage. She thought about going over to pick up the morning newspaper, but then she remembered Alice telling her that she'd stopped her subscription in favor of reading the news online. Annie could understand her reasoning but still preferred holding the real thing as she read. Somehow, she thought Seneca would appreciate that.

Her vegetables gathered, Annie paused to pinch off a few sprigs of mint before returning to the kitchen to rinse off her bounty. The mint would be perfect for some refreshing ice tea after the walk she and Seneca planned to take. As she stood by the sink, Boots glided into the kitchen on light feet and rubbed against Annie's ankles. Careful not to sprinkle the water-phobic cat with her wet hands, she blew kisses downward. "Good morning, sleepyhead. Would you like some zucchini blossoms in your morning kibble?"

In response, the feline sat back on her haunches and leveled an indignant stare at Annie. "You look almost as miffed as you would if I had doused you with the sprayer," Annie playfully chided. "I'll take that as a no on the blossoms." With a meow sounding more like "meh," Boots moved away from Annie to the food bowl and was soon consuming her breakfast.

"I'll leave you to dine in peace, but I'll be back as soon as I'm showered," said Annie. "Be warned." Leaving the vegetables to dry, she bounded upstairs to make herself more presentable after her time in the garden.

Two hours later she and Seneca sat back in their chairs, nothing but crumbs remaining on their plates, to enjoy their second cup of coffee.

"That's the first time I've ever eaten blossoms, of any kind, in my breakfast," Seneca declared. "I'm surprised I liked them, but I did. How creative of you, Annie."

Annie lowered her mug. "I'm not the creative one in this instance; Gram was. I never would have thought of using them if I hadn't found an entry in her garden journal about different ways to use zucchini blossoms and other edible flowers."

"What a wonderful heirloom that must be," Seneca said, looking around the charming kitchen. "Grey Gables feels like it's full of curios and history."

Thinking back on the different mysteries she had inherited along with the old home, Annie couldn't keep from grinning. "You can say that again. When I tried to take inventory after Gram died, I was totally overwhelmed. I even thought about hiring one of those professionals who catalog estates, but I'm so glad I decided not to. I would have missed out on so much satisfaction and discovery."

Annie had not expected those discoveries to span such a wide range of experiences, not only for her, but many of her Stony Point neighbors. But in time, she'd decided to embrace whatever secrets she found, to the happiness and relief of some and to the chagrin of others.

"Ah, the infamous mysteries," Seneca said. "Any unsolved ones you're working on now?"

"No. Nothing at the moment." Annie stood and gathered the breakfast plates to carry to the sink. "Of course, I haven't been to the attic in a while. Too busy in the garden and enjoying the warmer weather." After lowering the plates into the hot sudsy water, she turned to wag a finger at her friend. "And don't go asking me to take you up there in search of a mystery either."

Seneca clapped a hand over her heart like a heroine in a melodrama and batted her eyelashes. All she was missing was the heavy eyeliner. "Who, me? What makes you think I'd do such a thing?"

"Yes, you." Annie leveled a merry eye her way. "Reporters are rather known for their curiosity, you know ... and with good reason. But I'm going to help you have a total break from your profession, as long as Grey Gables will cooperate." Her face tilted upward toward the ceiling. "Hear that, house? We have entered a mystery-free zone until further notice. Preferably after the harvest."

Seneca lifted her mug to drain the last of her coffee. "Obviously, I made the correct decision in coming here for my vacation." She glanced at Annie's mug to make sure it was empty also and then carried both over to the sink. "Are we almost ready to head downtown?"

Swishing thoroughly around the inside and outside of the mugs with a dishcloth, Annie glanced back at the clock on the wall and nodded. "The shop opens at ten, so if we walk we'll get there just as Mary Beth or Kate is unlocking the door."

"It's a good thing crochet supplies don't tend to be

heavy." Seneca wandered over to the back window, gazing out at the bright day. "What a pleasure to be able to walk around all day in June without risking heatstroke."

Annie chuckled. "You should have seen the bemused looks on my friends' faces during my first summer here. I couldn't stop exclaiming about the cool mornings and how quickly the heat waves came and left."

"I suspect I'll be seeing some of those same looks while I'm here. Yesterday, I was too busy marveling at the fresh lobster and all the sea glass we found, but I'll be gushing about the weather the rest of the time I'm here. How can I not?" Seneca turned away from the window as Annie set the last of the clean breakfast utensils on the drying rack.

After wiping her hands, Annie and Seneca slipped into light sweaters and left Grey Gables. As Annie had predicted, they approached A Stitch in Time just in time to see Mary Beth changing the shop's sign from "Closed" to "Open."

"Good morning, Mary Beth! I've brought you a new customer." Annie's voice sang out. "This is my friend Seneca—"

The stocky woman winked at the two women and added, "Who is from your hometown in Texas and met you while writing a newspaper article about the car dealership." She extended a hand to Seneca. "I'm pleased to meet you, Seneca, and I hope you'll take to crochet as well as Annie did."

Seneca's eyebrows rose slightly, and she looked like she wanted to laugh but thought better of it. "I haven't lifted a needle of any kind except a couple attempts to replace buttons on my husband's shirts. He finally told me to find a seamstress, so I'm not sure Annie knows what she's gotten herself into. But I'm willing to try."

Mary Beth laughed, and her dimples made her look ten years younger. "No worries, we've had harder cases than yours in this shop over the years and still managed to teach them some skills. You'll come to the Hook and Needle Club meeting with Annie tomorrow, won't you?"

Annie hadn't mentioned the meeting to Seneca yet. Since she didn't want her friend to have anything remotely feeling like pressure during her time of rest, she'd decided to see how well Seneca took to the handwork before suggesting the meeting to her.

"Maybe we should give Seneca a chance to try out her purchases before signing her up for the club," Annie politely suggested.

"Of course." Mary Beth ushered them into the shop. "We'll pick out everything you need to get started, and we'll be here tomorrow, should you want to meet some of the other crafters. We also have women who are expert knitters and quilters, in addition to crocheters."

Annie pointed at an antique dress form that displayed a sleeveless dress and delicate cropped jacket in soft summer colors. "Seneca, I can't wait for you to meet Kate. She's one of the most talented designers I've ever seen. Both of those pieces are hers."

Seneca's eyes moved from the baskets of yarn in a plethora of hues and textures to the ensemble. "Oh, they're gorgeous!" She stepped close to the form, examining each piece. "I simply can't fathom the skill it would take to make something like this."

A quiet voice spoke from the other side of the aisle. "It's really just a God-given talent."

Annie turned. "Seneca, this is Kate Stevens, resident designer at the shop."

"God-given talent still has to be cultivated," Seneca told the younger, dark-haired woman. "These pieces are exquisite."

"I'd be happy to help Annie teach you to crochet. After all, it was her grandmother Betsy who taught me." She adjusted the jacket over the dress on the form and stepped back to assure herself that the combination hung perfectly straight.

"I didn't realize your grandmother crocheted, Annie." Seneca squinted, thinking. "Wasn't she famous for her cross-stitch, like those beautiful ones hanging in Grey Gables?"

Mary Beth answered for Annie. "Betsy was certainly famous for her cross-stitch, but she was also an accomplished crocheter."

"Betsy shared her time and talents so generously," added Kate quietly. "Even with a knock-kneed, fumble-fingered twelve-year-old."

Seneca looked back and forth between the craftswoman and her handiwork, and then she shook her head. "I'm finding it hard to picture you as ever being fumble-fingered, Kate, but I'll grab onto the hope that even I might be able to learn enough to enjoy the art of crochet."

"There's always hope." Annie threw an arm around her friend. "Come over here and let's get everything picked out for you."

The front door opened, bringing more customers. "Excuse me," said Mary Beth. "If you have any questions, I'm sure Kate will be able to answer them."

"We're starting off simple," said Annie. "I'm sure we'll be fine, so don't let us keep you from your other work, Kate."

Kate nodded. "OK. I'll be behind the counter, if you need anything." She smiled at Seneca. "Pick out your favorite color for the yarn, it always makes the awkwardness of starting more fun."

"Favorite color or colors, and fat yarn," added Annie. "Fat yarn is easier to handle at first."

"Then point me to the fattest yarn in the store!" Seneca grinned as she wandered along the displays of yarns, reaching out to test the feel of different skeins. "I think I'm beginning to understand what women mean when they talk about fiber therapy."

"And they're not talking about eating more fruits and veggies!" Annie laughed. She perused a display of crochet hooks. "For your first projects, pick a yarn that's not too fuzzy or lumpy. It makes it easier to see exactly what you're doing. Then you can move onto funkier yarn once you've got all the foundational stitches under your belt." She plucked a few different hooks from the selection.

"Thank you for assuming I will get those stitches under my belt." Seneca pulled a skein of variegated sunrise colors and brought it to Annie. "How's this one for my starter?"

Annie fingered the yarn. "Love the colors! You have a good eye, Seneca. I might just have to figure out something to make with it too. This should work great for you, and it's soft, which is always a bonus."

"May my fingers work as well as my eyes," Seneca murmured, as she looked at the hooks in her friend's other hand. "How many hooks do I need?"

Annie fanned the hooks out for Seneca to see. "Just one to start, but there are several kinds to choose from, depending on how each feels to you." She demonstrated the usual position the hook would have in Seneca's hand, and one by one she gave the hooks to try. "Do you have trouble with carpal tunnel? Mary Beth carries a wonderful set to ease the discomfort from those kinds of conditions."

"I don't yet, but it's good to know the option is available," Seneca answered. "With all the typing I do, I keep expecting the pain to come along." Handing the last hook back to Annie, she ran her gaze across the collection of hooks. "And the winner is … " She grabbed a blue aluminum hook and flourished it. "This one!"

$-8-$

"Oh no you don't!" Annie scooped Boots's lithe form off Seneca's lap. "Beginner crochet lessons and curious cats don't mix. Find somewhere else to go, or I'll have to shut you in the library." She kept her voice stern but also stroked the fur between the cat's ears with a gentle touch. Then, walking into the center hall, Annie released Boots and stood a moment to see where she would go.

The gray cat pointedly sat at the bottom of the staircase, taking time to lick a paw and rub it over her head, again and again. Once her grooming was apparently set to rights, Boots bounded up the stairs with her nose in the air.

Annie sidled over to the living room, where Seneca stood just inside the door peeking around the molding and trying not to giggle. "You saw that, huh?"

"Boots is so human, I think she needs a Social Security number." Seneca watched until the cat's tail disappeared at the top of the stairs, and she then returned to the couch. "She rather reminds me of my Aunt Thelma."

Annie followed her, removing the yarn from the bag embossed with the logo from A Stitch in Time, which lay where she had dropped it earlier to grab the cat. "So you had some characters in your family too?"

"You can say that again." Seneca nodded at the yarn. "Now, tell me what I do first. After that amazing walk to see the seals, and the delicious lunch at The Cup & Saucer, I'd better get my hands and mind moving, or I might doze off on you."

Looking at her friend's face and body language, Annie was pleased to see signs that Seneca was starting to truly relax a bit. Maybe she had misunderstood her behavior, after all, and nothing was bothering her except overwork.

She held out the yarn to Seneca. "We'll head out to the porch soon, but the first thing we need to do is to wind the hank into a ball. That's probably best done indoors."

Seneca eyed the bundle of yarn. "Hank? I thought yarn came in skeins. It looks pretty tidy as it is. Why bother making it a ball?"

"Yarns come in skeins and hanks and balls. Hand-dyed yarn often comes in hanks like this." Annie settled on the couch and patted the cushion beside her. When Seneca was seated, she launched into her fiber lesson. "At first glance, it does look easy to use. But you're sure to notice a difference as you crochet. Non-balled yarns tangle easier, especially near the end, and they make it more difficult to control the degree of tension."

Seneca nodded solemnly. "Hmmm, considering how much trouble I had with my thread knotting while just trying to replace a simple button, you've convinced me."

"You can buy a yarn winder at most yarn shops. Mary Beth carries them, but I find yarn winding to be very relaxing. I like to turn on some music and wind away."

Seneca rolled the hank around in her hands. "Sounds like something I can do while figuring out article hooks." She saw the puzzled look on Annie's face at her use of the term. "You know, the opening paragraph that grabs the reader and makes them want to keep reading."

Annie tossed her head at the reminder, embarrassed. "How could I forget? One would think I slept through my college composition classes."

"I'll bet you remember more facts from your math and accounting classes than I ever will, Annie! Especially accounting, since I steered a wide berth from those kinds of subjects, if they weren't required." Seneca laughed. "Should I take the wrapper off the hank?"

"Yes. Then carefully unroll it." Annie held out a hand for the thick paper once Seneca had peeled it off. "Be careful not to tangle the strands."

"I'll try." The dubiousness that tinged her face changed to surprise as she examined the bunched yarn. Her gaze following the twisted strands, Seneca saw where it went and carefully freed the looped end.

"Good, hold it up and it'll unwind naturally," Annie instructed.

Seneca lifted the hank higher and watched the yarn lengthen into a large coil. "People always tell me how observant I am, but somehow I didn't notice this was made up of something looking like a deflated inner tube."

"It's a lot prettier than an inner tube, though," Annie added. "See where there are two spare strands of yarn tied around the hank?"

After locating the ties, Seneca nodded.

"I'm going to show you what to do when you're balling yarn alone," Annie told her. "There are a couple ways I do it. One way is to drape the skein over one arm, like this." She took the yarn from Seneca, making sure she didn't tangle the strands, and slid the loop over her forearm until it dangled behind her wrist. "But the easiest way for a beginner, I think, is to use your knees." Annie sat straight, with her legs about six inches apart and her knees bent at a ninety-degree angle. She put the "inner tube" over her knees. "Position the two tied places where it's easy to reach them." After pointing out the ties, she tapped her friend's knees. "OK, it's your turn."

Once Seneca had positioned her legs, Annie transferred the yarn to her. "Now untie them." As Seneca removed the two spare lengths of yarn, Annie told her, "Some people will tell you to use one or two chairs or a winder, and you can, but I tend to keep to the KISS method."

"Would that be Keep It Simple Sweetie—or Stupid?" Seneca quipped, bending closer to the yarn as she picked a knot apart.

Annie winced. "There's no way I'd ever call you stupid. You know, Gram had a particular dislike of that word, and I always have too." She paused a moment, thinking. "Well, once I was, say, eight years old."

"I agree," said Seneca. "The sad thing is a word I almost never use to describe another human being, I'll call myself much too often when I don't live up to what I want to be."

Annie cocked her head. "Typical of perfectionists everywhere, I think. Once Wayne heard me mumbling to myself after I'd dropped a pan of cookies on the floor. He knew I was pretty critical of myself and reminded me how much I had grown in extending grace to others. Then he suggested it was time for me to treat myself the same way." Annie stared across the room like she was gazing into a time machine. "I learned a lot from him."

"We were both blessed in the marriage department." Seneca took a deep breath. "What's next? With the yarn, that is."

Annie shook herself out of her reverie and continued her lesson. "Locate the two ends of the yarn. Sometimes they'll be tied and you'll have to cut or unknot them."

Seneca once again examined the yarn. "OK, here's one, and ... here's the other. They're loose."

"Good." Knowing her friend was right-handed, Annie instructed, "Hold out your left hand, with all the fingers except the thumb together and straight out. Kind of like you're about to shake someone's hand."

Seneca followed the instructions, and Annie nodded. "Lay an end across your four fingers and wrap the yarn around your hand several times."

"How many are several?" Seneca asked as she started looping the yarn around her fingers with her right hand.

"Somewhere between ten and fifteen. Or twenty." Annie chuckled. "It's not an exact science. The important thing is to keep the yarn neither too tight nor too loose."

Seneca remained silent until she considered the amount of yarn around her fingers to be enough. "Got it."

"Next, you take the loops off your fingers and fold it in half, holding it in place between your thumb and fingers." Annie kept her eyes on what her friend was doing, to give correction in case it was needed. But it wasn't. "See? You're not nearly the handwork klutz you think you are."

Shooting her friend a comical look, Seneca answered,

"Shouldn't you reserve judgment until we have a usable ball completed?"

"Noooo," Annie pursed her lips as she drew out the word. "If I need to revise my perception later on, I can." Not that she had any intention of informing her friend, should she find the need to do so.

"I'm about to give my fingers cramps, I'm holding this wad so tight." Seneca winced. "Quick, tell me what to do next."

Annie patted her arm. "That 'wad' becomes the center of your yarn ball, and a death grip is not necessary, so you can relax. When you're making a yarn ball, looseness is a virtue. Stretched yarn makes for an unhappy crocheter."

"OK. But if I end up dropping the ball, you get to chase it down."

"Deal. Now, start wrapping the yarn over the wad until there's more bulk to work with."

Seneca frowned at the yarn pinched between her fingers. "But then I'll have to let go, and it'll unfold."

"No, you don't. Just continue wrapping the yarn around both the wad and your fingers, and then slip your fingers out when the ball is big enough to start turning it." When Annie saw the frown still in place on her friend's face, she added, "I'll let you know when it's time for you to start turning. Wrapping around your fingers will keep the yarn from being stretched too tight."

Seneca's mouth relaxed. "Good." Her right hand started wrapping the yarn until she felt a tug. "Oops. It's caught on something. What did I do wrong?"

"Not a thing," Annie assured her. "You just need to unwind another loop from the hank with your left hand." It had been so long since Betsy had taught her how to ball yarn, she'd forgotten the awkwardness she'd experienced as a beginner.

Seneca snickered. "Oh, I see." She followed the yarn in her left hand around her knees to unwind the loop. "I'm feeling a little sheepish."

"You realize if you had picked out alpaca wool, your pun would be a failure." Annie couldn't hold back a smile.

Seneca started wrapping the length of yarn she'd just released. "That's a relief, since I had no idea what kind of fiber I was touching. I only knew it felt soft."

"Your instincts, or your fingertips, served you well. I really like what you selected," Annie told her as she kept an eye on the growing collection of yarn on Seneca's fingers. "OK, you've got enough on your fingers. Slip the yarn off, turn the ball, and continue wrapping. It'll start looking more like a ball soon."

Doing what Annie had instructed her, Seneca considered her handiwork as she turned and wrapped. "Looks kind of sloppy, doesn't it?"

"You can worry about perfection later, right now the important thing is keeping the yarn loose. You're doing fine." Annie reached into the shop bag once more. "In fact, you're doing so well, I think I can wind my new yarn too." She pulled out a skein that was the color of poppies.

Seneca leaned over to get a closer look. "Wow, that's some mighty thin yarn. Almost looks like thread. What are you making with it?"

"Hairpin lace," Annie answered. "A while ago, I found a hairpin fork in Gram's sitting room. I'm finally going to give it a try, and if it's successful, I'll make some hairpin lace to trim a skirt for Joanna."

Seneca turned a puzzled look toward her friend. "A hairpin fork? I've heard of several kinds of forks but not a hairpin one."

"I wasn't sure what I'd found either," Annie confessed. "Gram never showed it to me when I was visiting her as a child. It took some digging to find some information about it, and how to use it. It was popular in the first half of the twentieth century, but it seems to be making a comeback lately from what I've read."

Turning and winding, Seneca nodded. "Sounds perfect for a vintage vibe."

"Exactly." Annie prepared her skein and started her own yarn ball. "I found some photos of a beautiful hairpin lace dress at a museum. If I enjoy the process, I might try to duplicate the dress or at least a blouse."

The women worked for a while in silence, enjoying the quiet companionship that comes from a longtime friendship. With her experience, Annie's ball was completed only a short time after Seneca's. Then they relocated to the front porch of Grey Gables, where a soft breeze kept them comfortable as Annie taught Seneca how to crochet a chain stitch.

A while later, Seneca leaned back in the wicker chair and sighed. "I finally comprehend your love of handwork, Annie." Lifting the long length of chain stitch she had crocheted, she smiled. "This is much more fun than replacing shirt buttons."

"I suppose it would be kinder to refrain from waving the I-told-you-so card at you." But Annie did not refrain from grinning. "So, do you think you'll be up for coming to the Hook and Needle Club meeting with me tomorrow?"

Seneca gazed out at the expanse of sea grass between the yard and the rocky beach as it swayed to the song of the breeze. "There must be something potent in this sea air, but I find myself looking forward to going tomorrow and learning some more." She laid the crochet on the table between the two chairs and stretched her arms. "But first, I plan to spend the evening catching up on some novel reading. I'm hoping that Stony Point will work its small-town magic on my tightly wound nerves."

"Oh, we have our pulse-pounding moments up here too," Annie said. "Just before I saw you Saturday, Alice and I almost were run over by somebody in a big, black SUV, and then we had a couple of guys show up at The Cup & Saucer who seemed suspiciously out of place. Still, a good book sounds like a perfect ending to the day. Can I make you some dinner first?"

Her friend's face took on a quizzical look, and then she shook her head. "Thank you, but I think I'll just have a small snack later at the hotel. I'm not remotely hungry yet."

"A snack ending with a chocolate or two, I presume." Annie cocked an ear toward the front door. After a moment of listening, she went to open the door and a gray blur trotted by her ankles and down the porch steps.

"Looks like Boots has lost her fascination for yarn." Seneca watched as the cat approached the wild grasses and stopped to nuzzle it. "Does she eat the grass?"

"I've never seen Boots actually eat it, and she's never gotten sick after being outside, either," Annie answered. "It appears to me that she just likes the sensation of the stalks against her face, kind of like a feline face massager."

The two women watched the cat for a few minutes until she disappeared among the wild rose bushes beyond the tall grass. Then Annie asked Seneca if she was ready to return to the inn.

"Yes, I'm looking forward to catching up on some fun reading, not just nonfiction or research." Seneca picked up the ball of sunrise yarn and her hook. "Should I take this with me?"

"If you'd like to, sure. Do you have a small tote bag for it?"

Seneca paused. "Well, I have a larger bag for beach and road trips. Not really anything smaller, except my purse, and there's no way the yarn will stay neat in there." She grimaced at the thought. "I should purchase something at A Stitch in Time tomorrow."

"Don't bother," Annie told her. "Grey Gables is a storehouse of bags of all sizes. I could almost go into business since I'll never be able to use them all. Come on. Let's find you one."

Seneca followed her into the large home and upstairs. Annie led her to the room where her grandmother had stored an amazing amount of handcraft supplies.

"Annie, the more I see of Grey Gables, the more I love it. Some Victorian-style houses are too froufrou for me, but this house is just right—interesting without being overwhelming."

Annie pulled open a drawer of the large oak dresser and started pulling out possible bags. "You should have seen me when I first arrived at Grey Gables. Oh, I was overwhelmed, all right." She held up two different bags, one made of blue-striped ticking material and floppy handles, and a green-and-blue one with stiffer handles. "Both of these have inserts for the bottom, so they'll stand up instead of slouching. That can come in handy." She handed them to Seneca and turned back to the drawer.

"How many bags are in there?" Seneca marveled as she stepped closer for a good look. "Did Betsy have a bag fetish or something?"

"Ha!" Annie chortled. "Not exactly, although she was definitely something of a pack rat. Gram was invited to teach at a lot of handcraft workshops and conventions, and every time she was given a bag as a souvenir." She handed a few more bags to Seneca.

Seneca examined each of the bags. "I like the ones with both firm bottoms and the non-floppy handles." She returned three of the bags to Annie, who settled them back in the drawer and considered the remaining choices. "This is the one for me." She displayed the green-and-blue bag with a flourish. "I feel like I'll be carrying you and Betsy with me."

"Good choice." Annie finished putting the other bags in the drawer, closed it, and then straightened. "We're honored to tag along."

After stowing Seneca's things in the bag and letting Boots back in from her meanderings, the two friends climbed into Annie's Malibu and watched the sun sink toward the horizon as they drove to Maplehurst Inn.

～ 9 ～

nnie brought the car to a stop under the awning of Maplehurst Inn and turned to her friend. "Do you want me to pick you up for the Hook and Needle Club meeting tomorrow, or do you want to walk?"

"I'll walk." Seneca snapped to attention. "Oh, I almost forgot. Would you come to my room for a minute? I have something for you."

"Sure, but you could give whatever it is to me tomorrow."

"I'll probably forget, like I did today. My brain is getting a little *too* lazy, even for vacation."

Annie nodded and shifted the car back into drive. "No problem." She maneuvered to the nearest parking space, and they exited the car. Smiling at the woman who ushered them into the lobby, the two chatted about the next day as they crossed the spacious room. Again, Annie was thankful to note the aura of relaxation about her friend. The combination of sea air and fiber-art therapy was doing the trick.

"Excuse me, Mrs. Marchal." Denise, who manned the inn's front desk most weekday nights, called as they walked past. Denise was a woman in her early thirties who wore a capable demeanor like perfume

Seneca's head swiveled. "Yes?"

"I have a message for you." Denise held a folded piece of yellow paper out to her.

Annie watched Seneca's face turn ashen as she hesitated before taking the message with a tentative hand.

"Thank you," Seneca murmured as she tucked the paper into her sweater pocket. She gave a quick nod at Denise and continued toward the stairs.

Annie laid a hand on her friend's arm. "Aren't you going to read the message? There might be an emergency." She thought of Alice and the calls she had missed from her sister the day before.

Shadows scuttled across Seneca's features as she slowly withdrew the note and unfolded it. Annie couldn't help but notice how relief flooded her eyes and posture. She managed a wry chuckle. "It's from Jake. Evidently he tried my cellphone and was worried when I didn't respond." She frowned and reached into her purse to retrieve the phone. After checking it, she looked up at Annie. "That's odd. It's muted. I know I raised the volume after church yesterday."

"It probably pressed against something else in your purse. I've had the same thing happen. If you kept it in your pocket, it would probably happen more often." Annie kept her tone light, although concern for her friend increased again after witnessing Seneca's reaction to the message. Was there any way to encourage her friend to share whatever was troubling her without scaring her into more silence?

Seneca nodded. "That's true. I get phantom calls from Hunt every once in a while. I even got a belt holster for his Christmas stocking, but he still just usually puts it in his back pocket." She glanced at the message once more. "I'll give Jake a call soon."

She pulled the key card from the front pocket of her

purse and opened the door to her room, ushering Annie inside the dark room. She flipped the switch on the wall to the left.

"How do you like your room?" Annie asked, taking in the elegant yet comfortable furnishings now that there was light.

Seneca set her purse and craft bag on a love seat placed at the foot of a four-poster bed, facing the fireplace. "It's charming—such a change from those cookie-cutter 'corporate' rooms in most hotels. The seating is actually comfortable too." She flourished a hand at the other side of the small couch. "Have a seat."

Annie glanced at the tall windows in the room, blinds down and curtains closed. "Don't forget to open the curtains early in the morning. You must have a spectacular view of the sunrise from here."

Moving over to a bureau sitting next to one of the windows, Seneca opened the top drawer. "It's a lovely way to start the day, as I did this morning. But I don't know if it's as comfortable as the view from your porch." She lifted a wrapped box from the drawer. "I tried moving the ottoman over to the window, but it sank down too low to see, so I just stood there like a statue for a long time."

"Then maybe you should rethink your plan and come stay at Grey Gables," Annie suggested. "You can sit and look to your heart's content—or until I put you to work in the garden." She relocated Seneca's purse and bag to the ottoman and patted the cushion next to her. "Have a seat." She wondered if her friend would open her windows to enjoy the cool evening air. To her, the room felt stuffy.

Sitting next to Annie, Seneca held the box out to her. "I couldn't come here without bringing you a little bit of Texas."

Eyeing the box, Annie considered what it might contain. "Looks a little small for a tumbleweed. We definitely don't have those up here, though I guess driftwood is the mid-coast Maine equivalent."

Seneca chuckled. "I'm surprised John and Joanna haven't tried to send you one yet."

"Now that you mention it, so am I!" Annie grinned. "I'll keep my eye out for a really large package come Christmas." She removed the green ribbon and slid a finger under the tape securing the paper dotted with different kinds of chili peppers. "Cute wrapping."

"I doubt you'll find it in any shop in Maine."

"You're probably right." Annie carefully tucked the paper beside her, lifted the lid of the box, and peering inside, clapped her hands and squealed. "Peanut brittle!" Lifting the three bags of brittle, she read the labels. "Oooo, peanut and pecan and ..." She gasped at the bag of brittle green enough for St. Patrick's Day. "Jalapeño! Won't that one be a surprise for my New Englander friends."

"Show them how Texans do brittle the right way," said Seneca. "There's something else in there."

Annie shuffled the bags of brittle around until she saw a lump of tissue paper. Nestled inside it, she found a plush armadillo. "Aw, what a cutie. Is it a nine-banded one?" She ran a finger along the ridged bands as if counting them.

"Look closely; it rolls up just like a real one."

Examining the stuffed animal, Annie figured out how to transform it into a ball. She held it aloft. "The next time

Alice comes over, I think I'll tuck this into my basket of yarn balls and see if she notices it."

"Make sure you let me know her reaction," said Seneca, smiling.

Annie settled the armadillo back in the box and reached over to hug her friend. "Thank you, Seneca, you are so thoughtful!"

Returning her embrace, Seneca spoke against her shoulder, "And thank you for introducing me to fiber therapy. I'm looking forward to tomorrow."

Annie leaned back as her friend let go. "So am I. My friends will have a chance to get to know you better." Her smile dampened a little. "I'm sorry Alice won't be there."

"I am too." Seneca stood to walk Annie to the door.

Annie gathered her box, tucking the wrapping paper inside. "I wanted to hear how her mother is doing today, but I didn't want to interrupt anything important." She better understood how her friends, including Seneca, must have felt when Wayne had been rushed to the hospital.

Seneca nodded in agreement. "Alice knows you're there for her. I'm sure she'll call when she is able." She opened the door and glanced out into the hallway. "Enjoy your evening, Annie."

"You too," Annie answered. "Tell Jake I said hi."

"I will." Seneca pointed to the box in Annie's hands. "I'd warn you to not eat all the brittle in one sitting, but I know you're more of a nibbler, unlike someone else we know."

"Hmmm, can't imagine who that could be." With a wink, Annie turned toward the stairs, hearing her friend's short laugh and then the closing of her door. She shifted her gift to one arm and glanced at her watch for the time. Should she call LeeAnn when she got home or before the club meeting tomorrow? During the summer, there was no such thing as regular free time for the mother of twins.

By the time Annie exited the inn into the pleasantly cool evening, she had decided to wait until the next day to call her daughter. Keeping the evening free to speak with Alice if needed seemed like a wise plan. Perhaps a cup of tea and some Texas brittle would be a tasty way to end the day.

*   *   *   *

Annie held her hands under the stream of water issuing from the kitchen spigot, thoroughly washing off the residue of soil from her time in the garden. She was pleased with how hardy her plants were looking and looked forward to a healthy harvest.

Glancing at the clock, she decided to phone LeeAnn since it was still early enough for the twins to be asleep. Annie retrieved a small breakfast of Greek yogurt and a half-empty jar of applesauce she had canned the previous autumn from local apples. She figured if she nursed the remaining jars wisely, there would be enough to see her through until the new harvest in August.

After dipping a portion of yogurt into a bowl and swirling in a generous dollop of applesauce with her spoon, Annie poured herself a cup of coffee and carried her breakfast to the table. She grabbed the cordless phone before settling into her chair and enjoying her first spoonful. The cinnamon sweetness sparked a shudder of pleasure through her, and she dialed her daughter's number with a satisfied smile.

"Hello?" Annie's smile widened at the sound of LeeAnn's voice.

"Good morning, LeeAnn! Did I make it before Camp Chaos begins?" Annie used the humorous code she and her daughter used to mean the busy summertime days with the twins.

"Yes, you did, though I can't guarantee how long we have before the campers charge in." Annie could hear the affection in her daughter's voice. As much as they joked about the challenges of raising the twins, there was nothing LeeAnn would rather be doing with her time. "Mom, I'm going to put you on speakerphone. I'm making some muffins for breakfast."

"No problem. This way you won't have to listen to me eating." Annie popped another spoonful in her mouth.

She heard a click and a slight echo as her daughter spoke through the speakerphone. "I'm not hearing anything, so you must be eating a quiet meal." The sound of a cabinet closing sounded.

"Yogurt and applesauce," Annie informed her. "I'll try not to slurp."

"Are you using the same kind of applesauce you sent us for Christmas?"

Annie thought back to when the weather had just turned crisp again and Alice had driven her to a pick-your-own orchard. "Yes. I was afraid I'd made too big a batch last autumn, but now I'm glad I did. I hope this year's apples are as good as last season." And she also hoped that Alice and her family were OK, as her friend had not yet called. "What kind of muffins are you making?"

To the sound of eggs being beaten, LeeAnn answered, "Blueberry with mini dark chocolate morsels."

"Ah, the twins' favorite."

"Yes. Although, I think I could leave out the fruit and they'd be just as happy." LeeAnn chuckled. Annie could hear the clang of metal measuring spoons. "But I took them to pick the blueberries, so John and Joanna will be excited to eat the fruit of their labor. Literally. What have you been up to? It's been a while since we've chatted."

Annie thought back over her last week and all the surprises it had held. "I know! There have been some unexpected things happening."

"Another mystery?" LeeAnn interrupted to ask.

"Actually, no. I'm sure that surprises you." Annie chuckled. "On Saturday when Alice and I were walking in town we bumped into Seneca Marchal."

"What?" Annie heard a clatter as a spoon fell into a glass mixing bowl. "You didn't tell me she was visiting."

"I didn't know! When I saw her walking along the sidewalk across from us, I thought I was hallucinating from the effects of a Pilates class."

The sound of stirring resumed. "How long was she in Stony Point? I hope you had some time to visit."

"She's still here. Evidently, she's finally realized she needs to take a break from work." Annie thought of the unusual ways her friend had been acting. "LeeAnn, don't read too much into this, but have you heard any news about Seneca recently?"

"How recently? And why?" LeeAnn sounded puzzled.

Annie thought a moment. "Oh, say in the last six to eight months or so."

LeeAnn was quiet for a while. Annie pictured her daughter dropping muffin batter into the tin rounds. "Off the top of my head I can't think of anything. Is there something wrong?"

"I don't know," Annie confessed. "Seneca just isn't completely herself, and I can't figure out why. Maybe she's simply tired—but then again, maybe not."

Annie could hear the oven door open and a pan slide in for baking. "Do you want me to ask around? Discreetly, of course. Maybe Herb has heard something; I'll ask him tonight." LeeAnn's husband occasionally ran into Hunter Marchal on a charity board on which they both served and might have another avenue for information that LeeAnn didn't.

"I'd appreciate that, honey," said Annie. "It might be nothing, but if there's something concerning Seneca, I'd like to help, if I can."

"Of course you do." Her daughter's voice grew tender. "You're like Spider-Man without the leotard. You can't help yourself."

Annie thought about how her core was still a little sore from Saturday's class and grimaced. "And without the muscles!" Before she could tell LeeAnn about her adventures during Pammy's class, she heard the sound of two whirlwinds blowing into the Sorensen kitchen.

"Hey, Mom, what're we gonna do today?" Eight-year-old John's voice was so loud it sounded to Annie like he was standing right in front of her.

The higher and slightly softer voice of Joanna chimed in,

"We can swim, right? What's in the oven?" Annie smiled at the energetic and curious voices of her only grandchildren.

"Blueberry chocolate chip muffins are in the oven and …" LeeAnn paused for effect. "Grammy's on the phone."

The crash of a toppling stool made Annie pull the phone a little ways from her ear. "Grammy! Let me talk to her!"

"Excuse me, young man?" LeeAnn's voice turned stern. Annie couldn't help but smile.

She could picture her grandson grappling with his impetuous nature. Then she heard him speak more carefully. "I'm sorry, Mommy. May I please speak with Grammy first? I want to tell her about Vacation Bible School."

"If it's fine with Grammy, I'm fine with you talking first since Joanna went first last time." LeeAnn had a steel-trap mind when it came to details. Annie's heart filled with thanks to hear another example of how her daughter had grown into a mature and loving parent.

"Yes, Grammy is fine with it," Annie confirmed. "And I promise not to wait so long to call next time."

"I might call you first," said LeeAnn, as she took the phone off speaker mode. "Especially if I find out anything about Seneca."

Annie carried her breakfast dish to the sink. "That would be lovely, of course. Have a fun day, LeeAnn."

"I'm sure we will. Bye, Mom."

"Bye, honey." Returning to the table to retrieve her coffee mug, Annie refilled it with the last of the coffee and carefully walked through the house and out onto the porch to enjoy her chat with John and Joanna.

～ 10 ～

The summer birds were still singing when Annie switched off the phone. She leaned back, the squeaking of the reeds of the wicker chair a welcoming sound to her. Perched at the top of the hill, Annie gazed over the panoramic view that Grey Gables afforded her. Annie reviewed her conversations with her grandchildren. How she enjoyed hearing about their activities, the different ways they looked at life, and the ways they described what they were learning at school and church.

Glancing at her watch, she realized she still had a good hour before leaving for the Hook and Needle Club meeting at A Stitch in Time. She watched the activity of the harbor as she considered what to do with the time. She thought of her request of LeeAnn to find out anything that might be bothering Seneca, and she realized she could do some online research of her own.

Annie hurried into the house for her laptop and returned to her wicker chair. She considered how differently she could do research now as compared to her college years, and she tried not to feel old. Launching a search engine, she typed "Seneca Marchal Texas."

As she ran her eyes along the search results, she murmured, "Seneca, my friend, you have been busy!" Scanning several announcements of awards and honors Seneca had won, Annie wasn't surprised. Her friend had always been a hard worker, and Annie knew she was well respected by both other journalists and also those in her community.

"But surely these awards wouldn't bring grief to Seneca," Annie reasoned out loud, as though conferring with Boots, who had followed her outdoors when she had retrieved her laptop and now lay curled on the cushion of the other chair. The cat's eyes were already closed and no help was forthcoming. "Some research assistant you are."

Next, Annie began exploring the archived articles of the *Brookfield Star*, the newspaper at which Seneca worked. After reading several of her friend's pieces, Annie realized how much her friend's work had changed over the years. Annie had always marveled at her writing ability, how she drew the reader into a story with her creative turn of phrase. Sometimes her features were long, and sometimes they were short, but Annie never felt like an article was a throw-away with Seneca, as it often was with other reporters and feature writers.

But the articles she was reading in the recent *Star* archives bore a much different focus and tone from the ones Annie had read every week when she had lived in Texas. Much more investigative in nature, her mouth almost dropped open as she read one about the origin and implications of illegal guns in Texas. The sources Seneca quoted didn't exactly sound like quirky artists or winners of Small Business of the Year awards. Annie had long admired her friend's intelligence and heart, but as she finished reading another hard-hitting piece, she couldn't help but wonder if Seneca had made some enemies with her pen—or rather, her computer.

"And LeeAnn gets worried when I'm working on a mystery!" Annie muttered as she glanced at the clock on her laptop. "That'll have to be enough research for now." She put the computer to sleep and reached over to rub the cat's ears. "Are you coming inside with me, Boots?" The gray ball of fur didn't move a twitch, just a brief opening of one eye. "I'll leave you to your dreams then."

She had deposited the computer in the library and was striding toward the stairs when her cellphone rang in her shirt pocket. Seeing Alice's name on the display, Annie answered. "You called just in the nick of time. I was getting ready to leave for the meeting."

"Annie—" Alice's voice wobbled and dissolved into weeping. "She's gone! Mother didn't make it."

Annie sat down on the step in the middle of the staircase, her knees weak. "Oh, Alice, I'm so sorry." She couldn't think of anything else to say in the face of something so weighty.

Her friend pulled in a shaky breath. "Her systems shut down so fast, the doctors couldn't do anything to stop it. She died early this morning. I've never felt so helpless in my life."

Oh, how Annie could relate to that emotion. It had overwhelmed her on the day Wayne had died and for many days following. "Alice, would you like me to come down?" She knew Seneca would understand if she needed to fly to Florida.

"Thank you for your willingness, but I think you should stay for Seneca."

Gently, Annie persisted. "Seneca's a big girl, Alice. I

know she would understand, and I can always spend time with her when I go visit LeeAnn and the family."

Annie heard a door closing on the other end of the phone, and when Alice finally replied, she dropped the volume of her voice. "I know this is going to sound weird, but I think Angela wouldn't react well to you being here. Of course, I'd want you to be with me, but Angela abhors talking 'family business,' as she calls it, in front of non-family members."

The term "family business" seemed a cold manner of describing a beloved mother, but Annie held her peace. Alice had long suffered an uncomfortable relationship with her sister. It saddened Annie that this tragedy had apparently only exacerbated the stiffness between them. She quickly considered how best to respond.

"The last thing I'd want to do is to make things harder for you, Alice," Annie began. "But please call me at any time, if you need to talk things out. I'll be praying for you throughout this."

Alice sniffed again. "Thank you, Annie. Will you let the girls know about Mother?"

"Absolutely."

"Good. I better let you go so you won't miss the whole meeting. I'll let you know the rest of the details as I can."

Annie glanced at her watch, relieved that she wouldn't be as late as she had first thought. "I'll get there just fine, don't you worry."

"OK. Bye, Annie."

"I love you, Alice," Annie reminded her friend. "I'll talk to you soon." She hurried up the rest of the stairs to her bedroom, trying to set the world record for changing clothes.

Seneca was pretty unflappable, so Annie knew she wouldn't panic when her only friend in town didn't arrive before the meeting began. But she was glad Seneca had had the chance to mingle with Peggy at the lobster bake, so she wouldn't feel like a total stranger. And, of course, Mary Beth and Kate were sure to be welcoming.

The busiest part of tourist season still being a couple weeks away, Annie was able to find a close parking spot in spite of her tardiness. As she jogged across the street to the shop, she waved to Jason, Stella Brickson's driver, but didn't stop to chat. Jason actually was much more than just a driver to Stella. He was personal assistant, house manager and confidant—her closest friend. Stella, the regal octogenarian who was also the de facto matriarch of the Hook and Needle Club, was sure to pass on to Jason the news about Alice's mother.

Entering the shop, Annie paused to calm her breathing before greeting the ladies gathered for the meeting in the circle of comfy chairs. Heads swiveled at her as she exclaimed, "I'm so sorry I'm late!"

"And on a week when you had a guest too," Peggy chided her friend with dancing blue eyes. "Tsk, tsk, Annie." The beginnings of a cheerful quilt with yellow and orange squares lay across her lap.

Seneca looked perfectly comfortable seated among the Stony Point residents. She had even chosen to sit next to Stella, a woman who sometimes gave off a less than welcoming air to newcomers. Smiling over at Annie as her friend took a seat, Seneca's powers of observation obviously kicked in, and her smile faded. "Is everything all right, Annie?"

"I just got off the phone from talking with Alice."
Annie settled her project bag next to her chair. "Her mother
passed away early this morning."

Death was always a hovering specter for those whose
family, friends, and neighbors had often made their living
from the temperamental ocean. As such, the Mainers often
sought to keep the proverbial "stiff upper lip." Emotions
were deep, but the outward reaction often was reserved.
Still, sadness flooded their faces as the news sank in.

"Oh, poor Alice," Gwendolyn Palmer murmured. "I wish
she wasn't so far away."

Peggy nodded agreement. "She should have her friends
around her."

Annie thought of her offer to join Alice, but kept quiet.

"We must send some type of a memorial gift," Stella
inserted, her fingers still knitting swiftly. "We want Alice to
know she is in our thoughts."

Gwen paused in her own knitting. "I'd be glad to order
some flowers. Any suggestions on what kind?"

Mary Beth nodded her approval. "Thank you, Gwen.
Does anyone happen to know if Alice's mother had any
particular favorites?"

Quiet settled over the group as the women combed
through their memories of Mrs. Robinson. Seneca bent
closer to her crochet as she came to the end of the chain,
as if trying to remember what to do next. Annie noticed that
after a moment her friend nodded to herself and managed
the correct steps to start another row. Seneca had been listening well during her lesson.

"I was not in Mrs. Robinson's social circles," Stella

broke the silence at last. "But lupines seem appropriate to honor someone from our beloved Maine."

Peggy looked up from the quilt squares she was sewing together. "I second Stella's suggestion. It's perfect. You can take the woman out of Maine, but you can't take Maine out of the woman."

"Also, Alice loves lupines, so it'll be like sending her hugs from all of us," Annie inserted. "Will they be available for delivery in Florida?"

"There's only one way to find out," said Gwen. "Do all of you trust me to select an alternative bouquet, in case they aren't?"

A look of amusement came over Kate's features. "Anyone who's seen Wedgwood and the lovely way you've decorated it would certainly trust you to pick out a floral arrangement." Her thin fingers moved a soft yarn of cerulean blue over her crochet hook with delicate skill. Gwen and her husband, John, the president of Stony Point Savings Bank, were pillars of the community and their home, Wedgwood, reflected their social status. The rest of the group nodded their agreement with Kate's assessment.

Gwen tilted her head graciously at the compliment. "I'll take care of it as soon as the meeting is over."

"I was thinking on the way here that it might encourage Alice if we all sent her occasional text messages," said Annie, pulling the hairpin lace fork and new yarn from her bag. "That way we don't have to worry about interrupting during inopportune times, and she can reread them as often as she needs or wants to."

Mary Beth immediately pulled out her cellphone.

"Excellent idea, Annie!" She stood and moved away from the circle of chairs, launching her phone's camera as she positioned herself. "I think we should send her a photo right now."

Instinctively, all the ladies glanced down at their clothes and patted their hair, with the exception of Stella. Then they scooted their chairs closer together before turning caring faces toward Mary Beth, who snapped a few frames. Alice's normal seat was conspicuously empty, a silent message to her that she was missed. "That should do it."

While the shop's owner concentrated on sending the photo text to Alice, the others returned their chairs to their original positions and continued with their handwork. Annie unwound a little of the poppy-color yarn and began to position it on the hairpin fork.

The movement of the fork caught Peggy's attention. "What's that you're doing, Annie?"

"Trying my hand at hairpin lace," Annie answered. "I found the fork in Gram's sitting room, and it's been calling to me for months now."

Kate smiled at her across the circle. "That might be the same fork Betsy used to teach me hairpin lace years ago. That yarn you're using is gorgeous."

"That's my strategy," Annie informed her. "Use a stunning fiber to distract from any imperfections of technique." Then her voice grew wistful. "How I'd love for Gram to be here to teach me too, Kate."

As the ladies' thoughts turned to Betsy, who had died a few years before, the feeling of the meeting turned toward the bittersweet. Annie contemplated the vibrant yarn she was manipulating with her crochet hook between the tines of the fork, picturing her grandmother's confident hands in place of her own. With her own mother dying of tuberculosis when Annie was a young woman, Betsy had been a vital influence in her life, every bit as vibrant as the yarn Annie was using.

Trying to shake off the melancholy, Annie told the group about the hairpin lace dress she'd seen online and how it was inspiring her current project, including the color. Then, Gwen asked Seneca to tell the group about her work at the newspaper. Annie listened closely for any clues in her friend's response, trying to hide her disappointment when Seneca kept her answer quite general in nature. Her friend seemed every bit the confident, energetic woman she had always known, which made those idiosyncrasies she'd seen over the last few days all the more puzzling.

Just as each member was tucking away her project, the text alert on Mary Beth's phone chimed. As she pulled the phone out of her pocket to check, Peggy leaned forward. "Is it from Alice?"

Scanning the message, Mary Beth nodded. "It is. Alice says to tell all of you that you're the best friends a woman could ever find." She glanced over at Gwen. "She also says the memorial service has been scheduled for Thursday, late morning."

"That's good to know," Gwen said, running a quick hand over her already neat chignon and standing. "I'd better get to the florist. I also have a shift at Ocean View this afternoon." For several years, Gwen had discovered much satisfaction in volunteering at the nearby assisted-living facility, just one of the many ways she served the community of Stony Point.

Peggy quickly stood, also. "I'll walk out with you, Gwen. I have to get back to the diner." She reached out to pat Annie's shoulder as she walked past her. "Thanks for giving us the news, Annie," she said. "Don't forget to bring Seneca by for some chowder soon. No one should visit Stony Point without having some of Marie's blue-ribbon recipe."

Exchanging a look with her friend, Annie nodded. "We'll be over soon, Peggy, so make sure you save some chowder for us. If Seneca doesn't mind, I'd like to pop over to Town Hall and let Ian know about Alice's mother first."

Seneca slid her new project bag over a shoulder. "That's fine with me. I enjoyed our last meal at The Cup & Saucer so much, I'm definitely looking forward to trying the chowder."

Peggy paused at the door just long enough to add, "See if you can convince Mr. Mayor to tag along," before sweeping out of the room on Gwen's heels.

Mary Beth and Kate both grinned at Peggy's command. "Something tells me that won't be too difficult, unless Charlotte has handcuffed Ian to his desk," the shop owner teased.

The meeting that had been dappled with shades of sorrow ended in a more lighthearted tone as Annie blushed and scurried after Seneca out the door.

~ 44 ~

"**I** apologize for being late to the meeting," Annie said to Seneca as they waited for the road to clear before crossing Main Street at Oak Lane. "I should have planned my morning better." She knew she should have stopped reading Seneca's articles earlier, but Annie wasn't going to confess to that particular detail.

Seneca waved off her friend's concern. "You had no way of knowing Alice would call this morning. I'm glad you were able to talk with her, instead of her having to leave a message or wait for you to call back." They stepped off the curb and strode across the street toward Town Hall. "Besides, you have nice friends. I felt very comfortable with them before you arrived."

Annie reached out to squeeze her friend's arm. "You're right; I am thankful Alice could reach me. But will you let me treat you to lunch, anyway?"

"If you must." Seneca donned a martyr's demeanor for a moment, but as they approached Town Hall her curiosity trumped humor. "I just love all the old architecture in New England's small towns." Her eyes drank in the historical details of the two-story white structure housing the city offices. "How old is it?"

"The town first developed as a port and trading post in 1665," Annie began reciting what she had discovered through her visits to the Stony Point Library, as well as the stories her friends had shared. "But between battles and fire damage, it's been rebuilt a few times." She paused to think a minute. "I think Town Hall was last rebuilt in the mid-eighteen hundreds."

"Not as old as the Alamo, then," Seneca commented. "What a shame fire and war took such a toll on the early buildings. Are there any structures left here from the seventeenth century?"

Annie gave a small shrug as she approached the double door and grabbed the handle on the right side to open and hold it for her friend. "I'm not sure. Ask Ian; he's likely to know."

"I will." Seneca stepped into the spacious center hall of the building and paused to breathe deeply, her nostrils flaring slightly. "I smell history."

Annie chuckled as she led the way toward Ian's office. "You look like Tartan when he's caught the scent of a cottontail."

"I've been compared to many things in my life, but never a schnauzer." Seneca leveled an amused look at Annie. "Just be happy I didn't smell mold or mildew, not an uncommon occurrence in old buildings, you know."

Annie gestured at the sign on a nearby door: Mayor. "Ian is pretty picky about maintaining proper upkeep of all the town's buildings. He's not a fan of fancy facades with crumbling foundations underneath." Opening the door, she ushered Seneca inside and greeted Ian's secretary as she closed it behind them.

"Hi, Charlotte. I'd like to introduce you to my friend

from Texas, Seneca Marchal. Seneca, this is Charlotte Nash. Ian couldn't do the great job he does without her."

The secretary flashed a welcoming smile, lighting her face under a short cap of silver hair. "I hope you'll enjoy your time in Stony Point, Seneca."

"Thank you, I'm quite taken with the town," Seneca responded. "If I didn't have a job and family in Texas, I might be tempted to become a snowbird."

Annie leaned closer to the desk. "Is Ian available? I have some news for him."

Charlotte picked up the phone's handset and pressed a well-worn button. "Ian, Annie's here with her friend Seneca." After a pause, she concluded with a simple. "Yes, I will." Including both women in her look, she told them, "You may go right in."

"Thanks, Charlotte," Annie said. As they approached the door, it opened, and the mayor welcomed them.

"And how are you ladies today? Did you have a Hook and Needle Club meeting?" Ian's warm brown eyes included both the women in his address, but his obvious affection for Annie was as bright as his gaze. He ushered them into his office and closed the door.

"We're both well, Ian." Annie couldn't help but hope she was answering truthfully for Seneca. "But we have some sorrowful news. Alice called earlier to say her mother passed away last night."

Ian stopped before he reached the chair behind his desk, the jovial look in his eyes changing quickly to concern. "What a shock for Alice. Mrs. Robinson had always been quite healthy, aside from her memory problems, as I remember. Had she weakened over the last year before the stroke?"

"Alice was never alerted to anything," Annie answered. "Shock is a very good word for what she's feeling right now." She gave Ian the information about the memorial service.

"I'll be sure to send my condolences and keep Alice and her family in prayer." Ian gazed at Annie, as if trying to gauge her emotions. "Will you be flying down for the service?"

Annie shook her head. "I think it would be harder on Alice for me to be there. And I sense her true mourning won't happen until she's back home in Stony Point." She hoped Ian remembered some of the history between Alice and her immediate family so she wouldn't need to elaborate.

Ian nodded. "You may very well be right."

"We stopped by for another reason also," Annie said after a moment of silence. "Seneca and I are having lunch at The Cup & Saucer, and we were wondering if you'd join us."

Seneca chuckled. "Consider it a special request from Peggy."

Some humor returned to the mayor's eyes. "That girl's a force of nature, isn't she? Let me check my schedule, but I think I can make it." He perused the calendar in his phone. "If you can give me a couple of minutes to make a quick call, I can take a break for lunch."

"Oh good!" Annie wiped imaginary perspiration from her brow. "Now Peggy will feed Seneca and me. We'll go chat with Charlotte."

She and Seneca scooted out of the room, carefully pulling the door closed behind them. Charlotte stood behind a worktable, box cutter in hand. She ran the sharp edge along the taped seams of a box and folded back the flaps.

Annie and Seneca sat down on an antique wood bench that stood against the wall opposite Ian's office door, but Annie didn't remain there long. Her curiosity, peaked by the stacks of colorful brochures the secretary was removing from the box, lured her to investigate closer.

"What are those, Charlotte?"

"New brochures for the Maine Eastern Railroad." Charlotte plucked a couple from the stack and held them out to her. "Here you go. Have you ever taken the rail tour?"

Taking the proffered pamphlets, Annie answered. "No, I haven't, but—" She turned toward Seneca. "This sounds perfect for a certain friend of mine who happens to love trains." Seneca sprang from the bench to join them.

"What's this about trains?" She looked over Annie's shoulder at the photo on the front.

Annie handed her a brochure. "The Maine Eastern Railroad runs up and down the mid-coastline. Would you like to go?"

"Of course I'd like to go." Seneca perused the information and photos. "There's just something about the word excursion that captures my imagination."

Charlotte glanced up from her work. "Then the copywriters did their job, didn't they?" She gathered up a couple dozen of the brochures from the stack and carried them to a display shelf hanging next to a map of Stony Point and the surrounding area.

"They certainly did," Annie murmured as she consulted the train schedule printed on the back page. "It just started

a daily run for the summer. Do you want to go tomorrow?"
She looked up at her friend.

"Where are you running off to tomorrow?" Ian's deep
voice spoke behind them.

Annie swiveled on her heel. "I was so engrossed, I didn't
hear your door." She held the brochure up for him. "Here."

"Ah, the Eastern Railroad." The mayor turned to
Seneca. "I highly recommend you take the trip. It's an
enjoyable way to experience the unique beauty of the coast."

Seneca grinned at his words. "You won't have to twist
my arm, Ian. I love riding trains."

Ian's gaze moved between the two women. "Would it be
imposing if I invited myself to join you?"

Annie hesitated, not wanting to answer for her friend.
Seneca glanced at Annie's face before asking Ian, "Can you
get away from your duties tomorrow?"

Charlotte had returned to her desk, and she consulted
Ian's schedule with the speed of honed experience. "Yes, he
can," she inserted, her friendly smile warming them all.

"It looks like we have ourselves an escort," Annie told
Seneca, pleased at her friend's reaction to Ian's suggestion.

Seneca clapped her hands. "I'm impressed. How many
visitors rate a tour of the coast with the mayor?"

Annie thought of the various honors she'd read about
earlier that her friend had received and almost said something about how hobnobbing with officials must be par for
the course for her. But since Seneca had not told her about
the accolades, she thought better of it. Instead, she drew
an arm around her friend and gave her a squeeze. "Only the
doubly special ones."

"I'll have to remember to tell Hunt that," Seneca replied. When Ian lifted an eyebrow, she clarified. "My husband."

Ian nodded and held an arm out to each woman. "Shall we go? We mustn't keep Peggy waiting too long, or we're sure to hear about it. Charlotte, would you like me to bring something back for you?"

"No thanks, Mayor Butler," the secretary answered. "I brought my lunch today and plan to have a nice picnic outside in the Town Square."

"Sounds like a lovely way to take a well-earned break," Annie said as she took Ian's arm. "Bye, Charlotte."

"Goodbye, Annie." The beep of the office phone interrupted the pleasantries. Reaching to answer with one hand, she shooed the three on with the other. "Keep going; I've got this."

Walking through the wide hallway of the main floor, Annie remembered the question Seneca had asked her earlier. "Ian, Seneca asked me if there were any buildings from the seventeenth century left in Stony Point, and I didn't know the answer. Do you know?"

Ian stepped before the two women to open the front door for them. "Seventeenth century … let me think on it a minute. At one point it was thought that the old Treadwell House was. But Liz Booth at the Historical Society consulted with an expert in period architecture, and apparently it's more likely to have been built sometime around 1740."

Annie and Seneca looked at each other. "Is the Treadwell House the oldest building here?" Seneca asked.

Ian nodded. "Of complete, fully standing buildings, yes. There are some interesting old ruins of small dwellings near the shoreline or on the property of some of the nearby farms, but I don't know how old they are."

"So the Alamo wins," Seneca teased. "Its construction started in 1724."

As they approached the intersection at Main Street, Ian nodded down Main in the direction of the old narrow brick building that housed the Stony Point Historical Society. "You'd need to consult with Liz to make sure of all the Stony Point facts, but I'd be surprised if there was a building older than the 1720s that I didn't know about."

A glint sparked in Annie's eyes and she turned to Seneca. "Would you like to pop into the Historical Society after lunch and confirm what Ian told us?"

"Absolutely," Seneca answered. "I'd love to."

The mayor looked first at Annie, and then Seneca, shaking his head with a laugh. "You two are quite a pair. Between the both of you, you've got more curiosity than a thousand cats."

"That's quite possible," Annie admitted, "unless you're talking about a thousand cats like Boots. If so, I'm not sure about that."

They had arrived at the diner, where Ian opened and held the door for the ladies. As Seneca stepped past the mayor, she aimed an impish smile his way. "Are you sure you know what you've gotten yourself into, escorting Annie and me tomorrow?"

"Probably not," Ian acknowledged. "But it's sure to be an interesting day."

~ 12 ~

The next morning, Annie stood on the porch of Grey Gables. As she waited for Ian to arrive, she watched Boots crouch motionless in the grass a couple yards from a small hole nestled among the clover. She knew something Boots didn't. The little striped chestnut chipmunk had already left its cozy burrow to find breakfast under the bird feeder.

"Your friend isn't home right now," called Annie across the yard. Once the small critter had come out of hibernation, the gray cat had taken great interest in her new neighbor, and Annie kept as diligent as possible to keep the chipmunk safe. Knowing Ian would arrive soon, she moved to the front door and opened it. "Last call, Boots, or you'll be out all day."

The sound of tires on gravel seemed to break the cat's concentration, and she finally peered around toward Annie. By the time the mayor's car came to a stop, Boots had jogged up the steps and into the house. Annie locked the door and slung her purse over a shoulder.

Ian met her at the foot of the porch steps. "You're as beautiful as the sunrise, Annie." He reached up to take her hand as she descended toward him and leaned close to give her a light kiss.

"Why, thank you, sir," Annie purred. She ran a light hand

over a sleeve of his shirt, the one she had given to him for his birthday. "You're adding nicely to the scenery yourself."

Ian covered her hand on his sleeve with his other hand and turned toward the car. It was a warm, comforting gesture. Opening the passenger door for Annie, Ian's glance was caught by the quick movement of the chipmunk as it dashed back to its burrow. "Is your garden suffering from critter invasion?"

Annie paused before getting into the car and followed his gaze. "Thankfully, no. Our little friend spends most of his time around the bird feeder. I've also sprayed a homemade repellent recipe I found in Gram's gardening journal. It seems to be working." She smiled as the chipmunk darted down the hole with bulging cheeks. She turned back to settle herself in the sleek automobile.

"If it's not too complicated, I think Becky could use Betsy's recipe," Ian told her as he buckled his seatbelt. "She was complaining last week of pests in her garden, rabbits to be exact."

"According to Gram, it works for rabbits and many problem insects, as well. I'd be happy to give Becky a copy of the recipe. It's quite simple, and I've not had any signs of rabbits nibbling in my garden." When Annie had decided to try vegetable gardening after moving to Maine, she'd not had one bit of confidence in her ability and had been completely surprised and delighted with her success. And now, thanks to Gram, she was even able to encourage Becky's efforts. Her grandmother would have been delighted too.

Ian lowered the sun visor as he turned the car toward the harbor. There was no telling what the weather would be like later, but the morning was a sparkling gem. "Thanks. I know Becky will be thrilled to find something that works. Did you hear from Alice last night?"

"No," Annie answered. "With the memorial service coming so fast, I'm sure spare time is rare right now." Her eyebrows moved toward each other as she stared out the windshield. "I hope she and her sister are communicating gracefully, and that Angela will keep Alice a part of all the decisions. I think it's so important for Alice to be completely involved."

Ian stopped briefly at the intersection of Ocean Drive and Maple Street and glanced over at Annie. "I agree, for both of their sakes."

A chiming emanated from Annie's purse. Pulling out her cellphone, she checked for messages. "It's a text from Gwen. Oh, she ordered lupines through Flora & Fern to be delivered to the funeral home in Florida, and they'll be there in time for the service."

"That will be comforting for Alice, I'm sure." Ian pulled up next to the front door of Maplehurst Inn just as it swung open to reveal Seneca, her hair framing her face and lifting as the breeze reached her from the nearby harbor.

In an instant, Ian had exited the vehicle, calling, "Good morning, Seneca!" as Annie waved to her friend from the passenger seat. "You and Annie picked a fine day for a rail excursion."

Seneca lifted her face and inhaled the cool, fresh air. "We certainly did! I can't get enough of early June mornings in Maine."

Ian opened the passenger door with a flourish. "They help balance the dismal days of February." After ushering Seneca into the backseat, Ian glanced at his watch as he returned to the driver's side. "We have plenty of time to make it to Brunswick and pick up our tickets before the boarding call."

"That means we can take our time and show Seneca more of the charms of Maine." Annie peered over the back of her seat. "I just heard from Gwen. She found the lupines for Mrs. Robinson's memorial service."

Seneca deposited her messenger-style purse next to her. "That's good news to start the day." Securing her seat belt, she leaned back against the comfortable cushion. "I'm warning you two. I need to do plenty of walking today after the delicious breakfast I just devoured in the dining room. I'm sure it wasn't as healthy as the one you made for me the other day, Annie."

"With the three-hour layover in Rockland, we'll have plenty of time for walking," said Ian. After checking for pedestrians, Ian pulled away from the inn, and soon, Stony Point was in his rearview mirror.

"Also, I have a *very* healthy homemade soup simmering in the slow cooker for us when we return," added Annie. "I thought the porch of Grey Gables would be the perfect place to share it at sunset."

Seneca's eyes were fixed on the display of countryside charms passing by the window. "I like the way you think, Annie. Of course, I always have."

"Will you be able to join us, Ian?" Annie asked. "I hope you don't have an evening meeting." She couldn't help watching his strong profile.

Ian turned his eyes on her just long enough to send a flush of warmth through her. "No meetings—that is, if you don't mind my dropping by the house to bring Tartan along."

Annie dipped her head. "We'd love to have Tartan, wouldn't we, Seneca?"

"Of course we would," Seneca turned her head briefly from the window. "He's quite the charmer, your Tartan. Unless you happen to be a red hot dog."

Even with the scenic route Ian took to Brunswick, the drive passed quickly, and Annie was a little surprised when they turned into the Union Street parking area. She and Seneca sat on one of the long white benches outside the station while Ian procured their tickets.

Seneca stretched out her legs, looking around her. "You know, I haven't been a huge fan of the current designer craze of painting everything gray, but I must admit the light gray clapboard with the crisp white trim does make for a charming train station."

A low rumbling alerted them to the approach of the Maine Eastern train, the dark green and white engine with yellow lettering pulling several refurbished Art Deco–era railcars. The two women watched as the engine crept past and finally came to a stop.

Ian joined them, tickets in hand. "We have reserved parlor class tickets. Plenty of space with great views."

Seneca flashed him an earnest bright smile, giving her companions a glimpse of the child Seneca had been. "Perfect!" she exclaimed.

As soon as the conductor announced the boarding call, Ian escorted Annie and Seneca to the parlor car. They spent the next two hours enjoying the scenery as they trundled across inlets and streams on bridges, watched ships being built in the boatyard in the city of Bath, saw lobstermen in their boats, and caught glimpses of a variety of wildlife. Annie couldn't help but grin at the sight of her accomplished Texan friend waving back at the children who waved at the train as it passed by small-town homes.

The train arrived in Rockland at precisely 12:25, allowing them three and a half hours to explore the quaint town and waterfront. As Ian had promised Seneca, they spent plenty of time walking before picking a place to enjoy lunch, and then they walked again, poking into whatever places struck their fancy, from artisan studios to antique stores, before ending their time in Rockland by visiting the Rockland Breakwater Lighthouse.

As they stood at the end of the mile-long breakwater, Seneca gazed around at the water, reflections of clouds scuttling across its surface. While she didn't say anything, Annie noticed her body language was conveying volumes, and she blessed Charlotte for opening the box of brochures when she did. This excursion was exactly what her friend needed. Ian kept an eye on the progression of the sun, finally checking the time before reluctantly suggesting they return to the station.

"Do we have time to make a quick stop in one shop on the way?" Annie asked him.

"As long as it's very quick," Ian answered.

Seneca dragged her eyes away from the water. "What shop?"

Annie chuckled. "You'll understand when we get there."

They made it back to the Rockland train station in plenty of time, Seneca swinging a large paper shopping bag from

Candy Haven with a contented look on her face. "This day just keeps getting better and better," she said as they settled into their parlor-car seats. "Remember when our kids would yell 'Sweet!' when they liked something—anything?"

Annie grinned at the memories. "Oh, yes. Over and over."

"This is one day when I think it actually applies." Seneca flourished her gift from Annie before placing it on the table in front of her. "Thank you both for this wonderful day."

* * * *

Arriving back in Stony Point, Ian parked so he and Annie could accompany Seneca into Maplehurst Inn. A mishap on the way to Brunswick had added the need for the quick stop before their dinner at Grey Gables.

"I'll only be a minute," Seneca assured them, shaking her head as they walked into the lobby. "All those train rides I've taken over the years, and I still managed to douse myself good. How embarrassing!"

Annie waved off her friend's chagrin. "Don't worry about it, Seneca, and don't rush on our account either. That soup's not going anywhere." A grin spread across her face. "Of course, if you'd like to join me at Pammy's class to work on your balance, I'd be thrilled to take you."

Seneca laughed and stepped closer to her, throwing her arms out wide as if to hug Annie close. "Such a wonderful friend!" Annie's sidestep to avoid her coffee-soaked friend drew another laugh as Seneca turned toward the stairs. "Y'all make yourselves comfortable."

Ian glanced around the room for available seats, his

eyes settling on a pair of overstuffed armchairs near the fireplace. "Those look promising." They had just settled into the comfortable seating when a shriek pierced through the genteel activity of the lobby.

— 13 —

"That's Seneca!" Annie gasped, pulling on Ian's arm and leaping for the stairs before the hotel employees had a chance to react.

"What's her room number?" Ian asked as they charged up the stairs toward the second floor. But when they reached the top step, they could see Seneca standing in the hallway about halfway down the corridor. She was alone, motionless and pale, her hands pressed against her mouth.

"Seneca!" Annie rushed to throw her arms around her friend, no longer worried about the damp shirt. "What's wrong?"

Trembling against Annie, Seneca waved a feeble hand toward her room and sputtered, "Snake! On the bed!"

"A snake?" Annie alone knew why Seneca was so frightened. Her friend was fearless about many things, but snakes were not one of them. Snakes were her kryptonite. "It should be OK. There aren't any poisonous snakes in Maine."

Seneca shook her head against Annie's shoulder. "Southern copperhead!"

"What?" Ian's head snapped toward the door. "How in the world—" Placing a comforting hand on both her shoulder and Annie's, he calmly asked Seneca for the room key. In a moment he had opened the door, retrieved Seneca's purse where she had dropped it, and had taken a good look at the thick-bodied snake curled up on the bed. As he quietly shut the door, the desk clerk and Linda Hunter, the owner of the inn, strode toward them.

The pair waited to speak until they were close to the distraught woman and her friends, trying not to alarm the other guests. "Mayor Butler, is everything all right here?"

"No, Linda, it's not all right. Someone has broken into Mrs. Marchal's room and placed a poisonous snake inside. I saw the snake myself."

The desk clerk stifled a gasp. "But we don't have poisonous snakes here."

"Which makes it plain that a security breach has occurred," Linda said, her usual warm smile replaced by a look of concern.

The clerk nodded. "Of course, you're right. Shall I call the Fish and Wildlife Service emergency number?" She glanced at her watch. "The office is closed for the day."

Linda glanced at her watch, weighing her options. It wasn't often wild animals strayed into Maplehurst Inn; in fact, apart from the odd mouse, it was a first.

Ian retrieved his cellphone. "One of the officers, 'Quill' Quillinan, is a friend of mine. Shall I call him direct and save us some time?"

Linda's hand dropped. "I like that plan, Ian. But let's all go to my office before you make the call."

Annie nodded toward Seneca. "I'm sure Seneca would appreciate a chair right about now."

"And how!" the visitor muttered, glancing once more at the door to her room before following the others down the stairs. She peeked around the spacious lobby as she descended, which thankfully was quiet like most midweek nights before the full tourist season.

Annie breathed a sigh of relief, both for the sparsely inhabited lobby and also for the way her friend's color was returning to normal—at least until they were almost to Linda's office. Then Seneca's face once again drained of color, and her features paralyzed. Annie slipped her hand into her friend's and raised an eyebrow and whispered, "What?"

Linda unlocked the office door, ushering them inside with a "Ladies, have a seat. Ian, you can grab that chair in the corner, and make your phone call."

As Seneca sank into the upholstered chair, she mouthed to Annie, "In a minute." Her friend gave a subdued nod in response and turned her attention to Ian's side of the phone conversation, as he remained standing beside the chair in the corner. Linda began making notes of the incident on a tablet.

"Thanks, Quill, see you soon." Ian ended the call, slipped the phone back in place, and relocated the chair next to Annie's before making his report. "He's grabbing a snake cage and heading our way in five minutes. Should be here in about twenty."

"Brit," Linda said, addressing the desk clerk. "I need you to stake out Mrs. Marchal's room. If you see any sign of that snake leaving the room, I want to know immediately."

"Right." Brit nodded briskly and left the room.

Linda turned her eyes on the remaining three. "Can I order any of you something to drink?"

"Some hot tea might be nice," Annie answered. "Seneca?"

Her friend nodded. "Yes, hot tea for me also." She glanced down at her blouse. "I've had enough coffee for today."

"Just water," Ian responded.

After calling the dining room to order the beverages, Linda's tone turned serious. "In my years here in Stony Point, much less at the inn, I've never run across a poisonous snake, and I have no reason to believe this was an accident. I also very much doubt the target is random."

Seneca reluctantly nodded.

"Mrs. Marchal, is there anyone you can think of who would wish you harm?"

"Not from here," Seneca answered. "But back in Texas, yes—though I had hoped it would blow over."

Annie leaned toward her. "Does it have anything to do with your investigative reporting?" Her friend's eyes turned to her. Annie answered the unspoken question, "Yes, I've read some of your amazing features. They're quite a bit different from your business profiles."

"This is making a lot more sense," Ian said. "What have you been investigating in the last six months to a year?"

Drawing in a deep breath, Seneca composed herself before answering. "My last investigation was about the illegal exotic animal trade. Texas is a major hotspot for that huge business."

"Illegal exotic animal trade? That makes the snake a less random object, certainly. You must have really ticked off someone."

"Can't blame this on anyone but myself," Seneca said with a wry shake of her head. A knock at the door stopped Seneca from continuing. The waiter was allowed inside to distribute the beverages. Once he had left, Seneca resumed her tale.

"I worked for months building trust with a man connected to the illegal animal trade, a bottom-pyramid kind of guy. Finally, I convinced him to tell me when and where a trade was happening so I could see one for myself."

"Did Hunt know what you were up to?" Annie asked, amazed at the heights of her friend's courage. And LeeAnn worried about *her* mystery research!

"Well ... not exactly," Seneca confessed. "I told him I was working on a big project, but that's all.

"The setup was going perfectly," she continued. "I went early enough to make sure I was hidden from sight but could still see everything and even record the trade. Until ..." A flush crept across her face. "I was caught by surprise when I realized how they had protected their illegal cargo."

Annie cocked her head, thinking of her friend's one greatest fear. "They didn't—"

"Yes, they did." Seneca huffed a sigh. "They were smuggling saltwater crocodiles but used a trick that I've since learned is a common tactic, which is to layer the contraband under a topping of dangerous cargo. I'm sure you can guess what kind."

Ian answered for everyone. "Snakes?"

"You got it. Venomous snakes, to be more exact." Seneca shuddered at the memory and then braced herself to finish the story. "I was so caught off guard, I gagged out loud. It was a completely spontaneous reaction, almost like someone else had gagged *for* me."

Annie clapped a hand over her mouth, thinking of the danger in which her friend had been.

"I was mad at myself, but I wasn't about to surrender. So

I scuttled out of there as fast and silently as I could. I kept expecting a bullet in my head at every step but just prayed and ran from hiding place to hiding place." Seneca paused to take a long, calming sip of tea. "It seemed so bizarre to me that I got away. For a while, I had myself convinced I'd gotten away with it—until the messages started coming."

Linda held up a hand. "Mrs. Marchal, before you continue, I think it's best we put a call in for Chief Edwards. I'm sure the use of a poisonous snake to intimidate and endanger a visitor to our town is something he'll want to investigate."

Seneca nodded. "Certainly. Obviously, the point where I can handle this myself has past." They paused their conversation until the inn's owner had contacted Police Chief Reed Edwards.

Replacing the handset of her office phone, Linda informed them the chief was on his way.

"Seneca, you used the word 'they,'" Ian said. "Do you know the identities of any of the people involved in the trade?"

Seneca's shoulders sagged. "No, I'm sorry, I don't. My contact would only give me the information if the traders remained anonymous, for both his protection and mine, whatever good that did after my stupidity."

"Do you still have the video of the beginning of the trade? Any decent head shots or identifying marks?" Ian was all business, while scenes of what could have happened to her friend kept unfolding in Annie's mind. She wouldn't have been surprised if her face was as pale now as Seneca's had been.

Seneca pulled her cellphone from the purse Ian had retrieved from the room and handed it across the desk. "I do, but I doubt it will be much help. It was a pretty dark place, and I had to run before I could get any footage of the crocs. I did get a pretty good look at the men and one woman involved, and I'm not likely to forget them, but it didn't come out well on tape. I needed better equipment."

After reviewing the video and showing it to Linda, Ian returned Seneca's phone to her, along with a fresh pad of paper. "I'm sure Chief Edwards will want to see this. While we wait for him, why don't you write as complete a description of those dealers as you can remember."

"That's a good idea, Ian," said Linda. "Then we can check with the staff and see if they remember anyone around today who might match one of the descriptions. We'll also make a copy for Quill and Chief Edwards."

Seneca filled out a page of descriptions. As soon as she handed the pad back to him, Ian asked, "Seneca, what kind of messages did you receive?"

"At first, I started getting hang-up calls at my office number," Seneca answered. "Didn't think anything of it at first. Sometimes people call and then think better of talking to the press and hang up before talking to anyone. Any newspaper reporter experiences some of that." She glanced sideways at Annie. "Then they started leaving voice mail for me when I was out of the office, mostly warnings to keep the information to myself."

Knowing her friend well, Annie said, "I don't suppose you asked the authorities to have the phone numbers checked."

"Of course I didn't." Seneca flashed a quick smile at her friend. "I didn't want to completely destroy my chance to still get a good story." She lifted her shoulders in a shrug.

"A bit naive, perhaps, but I still hoped the traders would assume their warnings had worked, and that I'd bagged the whole thing."

"But they didn't," Ian murmured to himself, and then he turned to Linda Hunter. "Any ideas on how to get Seneca to a safer place without her being trailed? We don't dare risk taking her anywhere in my car now, as the person may have been monitoring the inn when we arrived."

"And might still be," Linda added, nodding. "It would be helpful to know if this is the work of one person or more. Mrs. Marchal's descriptions are helpful, but we have no guarantee the culprit here was also at the trade. It could be some lackey." Then she asked Seneca, "Have you heard anything from your informant since the night of the trade?"

Seneca shook her head. "He's laying low to protect himself, I'm sure. Wouldn't be surprised if I never hear from him. I haven't tried to locate him again, for both of our sakes."

"Under the circumstances, I'd say you made a wise choice." Ian was interrupted by a brisk knock at the office door. "That's probably Quill and Chief Edwards." Ian strode to open the door. "Thanks for coming, Quill, Reed. I sure appreciate your quick responses." Stepping back, he made room for the police chief and then Quill and the cage Quill carried.

"No problem, Ian. It's not every day I get to wrangle a pit viper." Quill acknowledged the two women, tipping his brimmed hat. "Ladies."

"Quill, this is Seneca Marchal," Ian said, as Seneca held out her hand. Glancing around the room, the muscular wildlife officer lowered the cage to the floor against the nearest wall, wiped his right hand against his pants, and stepped to shake the reporter's hand.

"Nice to meet you." The wildlife officer managed a brief smile before releasing Seneca's hand.

Quill was a man of few words, and Ian knew it, so he quickly continued. "And I don't think you've met Annie Dawson before, have you?"

Annie's bright smile radiated her appreciation. "Hi, Quill. I'm sorry we interrupted your dinner."

"No problem, I'm a fast eater anyway." Quill gave Annie's hand a quick pump before getting down to business. "So where was the snake last seen?"

"Seneca, this is Chief Edwards," Ian finished his introductions before addressing his friend's question. "Reed, I could show Quill the room while you talk to the ladies. I assume you'll need to figure out a way to get Seneca away from the inn," Ian said.

"Just don't try to do Quill's job for him, Ian," Annie said.

The mayor held his hands up in surrender. "Don't worry. I can barely keep Tartan in control. I have no desire to try my hand at a poisonous snake."

Annie's body relaxed as she heard Ian's promise, freeing her mind to focus on Seneca. She gave Ian a quick smile of encouragement as he left the office with Quill, cage in hand. Then she turned back to address Linda and Chief Edwards.

"I would like Seneca to stay with me at Grey Gables. Do you think she would be safe there?" She noticed her friend opening her mouth to protest. "Seneca, I know now you originally refused to stay with me in order to protect me, but I can't help but think public lodging is not the answer anymore."

The rumble of a cart as it passed the office door sounded as Linda offered her opinion. "Chief, one downfall of public lodging is the need to keep an atmosphere of calm for the other guests. From that perspective, I think Grey Gables may be a better choice, as long as we can get Seneca there without anyone noticing. What do you think is best?"

"Oh, Annie, I never wanted my visit to put you in danger." Seneca dropped her face into her hands. "I was so careful while I drove here, using cash for everything. How did they figure out I was in Stony Point on the other end of the country?"

Annie leaned close to her friend. "Seneca, you aren't responsible for the actions of others, and let's not jump to conclusions about my safety. Chief Edwards knows what he's doing. He'll help us figure out what we should do to protect both of us." She ran her hand gently across Seneca's hunched back, trying to help her relax.

"Mrs. Marchal, I can assure you we'll do everything possible to keep both you and Annie safe." The chief's calm and capable tone was honed from many years in his career.

"And they've had a bit of practice with me," Annie reminded her friend.

Seneca raised her head, smiling her thanks at Annie as her friend removed her hand. "Thank you, Chief Edwards. I'm feeling better now."

The inn's owner stood and moved away from her chair, gesturing for the police chief to take her place. Edwards nodded and took the seat, pulling a pad from his shirt pocket. Linda took the page of descriptions Seneca had written to a small copy machine in a corner to prepare several copies.

"Good. Before I consider the question of your reloca-tion to Grey Gables, I need to get more information from you, Mrs. Marchal." The chief asked Seneca to repeat the events leading up to the discovery of the copperhead.

"How much information does your informant have about you?" Chief Edwards asked Seneca after hearing about her source within the endangered animal trade. "Could he be involved in this harassment by the dealer?"

"I didn't give the informant any personal information about me, but it doesn't mean he didn't ferret some out elsewhere."

"So, do you think he could have led the dealer to you?" Chief Edwards leveled his intense eyes at her. "How do you know the informant wasn't a plant?"

Seneca squinted at the chief, setting her two worry lines slanting toward each other. "What possible motive would a dealer have to send someone to an investigative reporter to target attention of their lucrative, illegal business? I just can't think of any viable reasons, can you?"

Edwards barked out a quick laugh. "No, I can't, but over the years I've seen far too many people do outrageous things for senseless reasons to rule the informant out. Just to clarify, you did not attempt to communicate with your informant after the night of the trade?"

"That's correct. I did not," Seneca answered plainly. "As far as I know, he has not tried to contact me, either."

The chief left that line of questioning, leaning back in his chair. "After hearing more, I agree with Linda about re-locating you. Grey Gables should work as well as any other place. Now, we need to get you and your belongings out of here without being traced. Annie, do any of your friends ever use Maplehurst's kitchen for catering?"

Both Stella and Gwen came to mind, but Annie did not feel comfortable even mentioning Stella. "I'm sure Gwen Palmer has, why?"

"Well, we both know she's someone we can trust."

Annie chuckled. "I would certainly hope so, considering my money is in her husband's bank!" She coughed, composing herself. "How does Gwen fit into your plan?"

"Good. Here's my idea." Annie and Seneca leaned forward to take in Chief Edwards's proposal, anxious to leave the inn, at least until the dealer's henchman had been caught.

— 14 —

By the time Ian and Quill returned to the office with the cage—draped with a sheet, so as not to alarm the other guests—most of the details of the transfer plan had been worked out and Linda had left to begin making preparations. With the whereabouts of the dealer's lackey unknown, Quill did not want to load the snake into his truck until he was ready to leave.

"I'm not going to lie," Seneca confessed, "I feel a little better since you added the sheet." She shuddered. "But not by much."

Chief Edwards stood. "Quill, you can use my desk to take Mrs. Marchal's statement for your records. I have a couple of details to iron out before we move the women to Grey Gables."

Ian's head jerked up, and he stared at the chief. "Are you sure that's a good idea?"

Annie laid a hand on Ian's sleeve. "Chief Edwards has designed a safe way to get Seneca there without drawing any thugs."

Ian frowned, obviously not convinced.

Chief Edwards strode over to the mayor, trading places with Quill. "Come with me, Ian. I'll give you the details while we sweep the inn for anyone matching the descriptions Mrs. Marchal gave me or anyone looking suspicious, for that matter."

"I'll come and listen, but I can't promise I'll like your plan," Ian said. "It's hard to accept any plan that can put our citizens and visitors at risk."

Edwards clapped a hand on Ian's shoulder. "Understood, Mayor. After you hear the details, if you have any better ideas, I'll listen. Now, let's go look around."

After a final look toward Annie, his eyes grave, Ian followed Edwards out of the room. The two women repeated the information for Quill and then answered the Fish and Wildlife officer's additional questions about how much Seneca had learned of the animal smuggler's operation.

At last, Seneca gave a small groan. "I've combed my brain for every detail, and I don't think there's another one in there. I hope it's enough for a start, anyway."

"Should be," Quill said. "My next step will be to get a special agent of the Environmental Conservation Police assigned to the case. Then I'll be contacting you with information about what we need you to do next. Until then, once Chief Edwards gets you settled, I need you to lay low, Mrs. Marchal. Stony Point's too small for you to be out and about. The risk is too great that the wrong people will see you. Oh, and don't use your cellphone until I tell you it's OK."

Seneca winced. "Can I still keep in touch with my family and editor? Hunt would go crazy if he didn't hear from me regularly."

"If the transfer to Mrs. Dawson's house goes smoothly, you can use her phone tonight." The agent turned to Annie. "But it would be better if you could buy her a burner phone tomorrow to use until we've put the lid on this dealer or at least his thug."

Annie asked, "What's a burner phone?"

Seneca answered her. "It's a prepaid phone you can use without needing personal identification or a contract. Why didn't I think to get one before I left home?" Exasperation built in her voice. "I should have known better!"

Quill tore a sheet from the pad. "I'll give you the names of some prepaid phones that'll work." He jotted down some names and held the list out to Annie.

Running her eyes down the names, Annie nodded. "Thanks, I'll get one tomorrow."

"Good. Text my cell number as soon as you have it, and I'll always contact you on that phone. Any conversation with anyone about this, including Ian, should be on the burner phone." He pulled two business cards out of his shirt pocket, handing one to each woman.

"I will." Annie glanced at the card before slipping it into her wallet.

Seneca was gnawing the inside of her cheek as she gazed at the card in her hand. "I suspect email is also out of the question?"

"Yeah, email's pretty easy to hack for the kind of people we're dealing with here." Quill sauntered over to the side of the window, brushing the curtain aside just enough to peer outside for a minute. He let the material drift back into place and turned around, checking the time on the nautical wall clock.

Annie was starting to get nervous about the time. Using the inn's catering van to transfer Seneca to Gwen's home, Wedgwood, wouldn't be very believable if it didn't leave until mid-evening. Then again, some gatherings over cocktails and hors d'oeuvres sometimes started rather late. Maybe it would be all right. Annie breathed a prayer and calmed herself, leaving their plan in God's capable hands.

Seneca jumped when the door of the office opened to reveal Ian and Chief Edwards. Turning a sheepish face to Annie, she said, "I've gone from fearless reporter to mush in no time flat! How embarrassing!"

"You have nothing to be embarrassed about, Seneca," Annie assured her before turning her attention to the men. "Any sign of suspicious characters?"

Ian shook his head. "Not a whisker."

"Doesn't mean he's not lurking somewhere close, though," Chief Edwards added. "We took the liberty of stopping by your room to pick up some items and clothes you might need. They're in cleaning bags in the kitchen."

"Reed thought it would be best if we left enough things, like your suitcase, in the room to make it look like you are still lodging there, in case the thug pays another visit to retrieve the snake," Ian explained further. "The bags will go with you to Wedgwood, and then to Grey Gables."

"Sounds like you approve of Chief Edwards's plan," Annie observed, relieved.

"It took some convincing, but I do understand the need for it," said Ian. "Since there aren't many options open to us, I have to admit it gives us the best chance of success. I'm thankful Gwen and John were at home tonight."

Quill tucked the paper with the information he had gathered away in a pants pocket. "I've given Mrs. Dawson and Mrs. Marchal instructions. I don't know who yet, but a special agent will be contacting Mrs. Dawson tomorrow."

"Special agent?" Ian raised an eyebrow. He turned to Annie. "That's a new one, even for you."

"Oh, really?" Seneca nudged her longtime friend. "Sounds like there are more stories for you to share while I'm in hiding at Grey Gables."

Annie shrugged modestly. "Well, maybe a couple."

"Or a couple dozen," Ian added, bringing a shadow of a smile even from the chief. Anyone who had lived in Stony Point for even a few months knew something of the mysteries the Texas transplant had the tendency to uncover.

Quill bent to heft the cage and nodded at Ian. "Get the door for me, will ya?" He looked over his shoulder at Annie. "Get that phone as early as you can tomorrow, Mrs. Dawson."

"I will," Annie assured him. "Thanks again."

After man and snake departed, Annie shifted in her chair. "I don't like the idea of leaving Seneca alone tomorrow to buy the burner phone. It feels like it will be too soon after the transfer to know if it was successful or not."

Chief Edwards's eyes moved between the two women. "Do either of you have an iPhone?"

"I do," answered Seneca.

"There's a burner app you can use to get a workable number that will last for twenty minutes or two weeks for a small cost. You can also buy new numbers if you need them. It is a way to use an unrecognizable number on your phone that can't be traced."

Seneca's face brightened. "Really? I had no idea! I'll download it as soon as I get to Annie's house."

Ian met Annie's eyes before addressing the chief. "Reed,

Annie doesn't use an iPhone. Do you think it would be wise for her to purchase a burner phone?

"It could be useful," said the chief. "Cover all your bases, so to speak."

"I can get one tomorrow morning and deliver it to you," Ian told Annie. "Perhaps at lunchtime?"

Annie nodded. "If you have the time, I'd really appreciate it, Ian. I'd feel better not having to leave Seneca alone so soon after the transfer."

"OK, let's get this show on the road," the chief declared. "If the thug left the premises and vicinity to escape detection after he planted the snake, he's likely to return within a few hours, assuming he's a one-man show."

"Or one-woman show?" Seneca countered. "The male gender isn't the only one involved in animal trafficking, I've learned."

"Fair enough." Edwards nodded before continuing. "Whatever the gender, we can't assume we have hours to relocate Mrs. Marchal. The sooner, the better."

In a gesture well known to anyone who ever attended Town Hall meetings, Ian squared his shoulders, as though readying for battle. "I agree. Just tell us what to do."

Like clockwork, the chief guided the steps of the escape plan until just thirty minutes later, a Maplehurst Inn catering van trundled up the driveway of Wedgwood, the stately home of John and Gwendolyn Palmer. It pulled around to the back of the house, where Gwen was waiting to greet the three members of the "catering staff" and usher them in through the back door. Forty-five minutes later, "guests" began to arrive: Kate Stevens, Mary Beth Brock, the Reverend and Mrs. Wallace, Todd and Becky Butler, Grace Emory, and Charlotte Nash.

After the impromptu party, during which Annie, Seneca, and Ian finally ate a delicious dinner of leftovers from the Palmers' meal and shared with their friends the sketchiest details absolutely necessary about the latest mystery, the guests began to depart. While the dark blue sedan of Charlotte Nash had gained two passengers, who remained slumped low in their seats for the short drive to Grey Gables, the Maplehurst Inn van returned to the door of the inn's kitchen with only the driver, Ian Butler.

Shedding his caterer's garb and before heading home, Ian popped into the inn's office where Linda and Chief Edwards were waiting.

"How'd it go?" Linda asked, rubbing an eye with a knuckle.

"So far, so good. I'm expecting Charlotte's report any minute." Ian pulled his phone from its holster.

"Notice any unfamiliar or rental vehicles while you were on the road?"

Ian eyed his phone, as if willing it to ring. "No."

Chief Edwards added some notes to his case file and then began tapping the file with the closed pen. The tapping continued until Ian's phone rang moments later.

"They're safe?" was the mayor's greeting to his secretary. He breathed in a deep breath. "Good. You've once again gone above and beyond, Charlotte. Thank you ... and please take some comp time tomorrow." He paused to listen to her response. "I really think you should, but the decision is yours. Have a good night." He closed the phone, staring at it a moment before holstering it. "Annie and Seneca are at Grey Gables. Charlotte escorted them inside. She stayed to help Annie and Seneca look around the house to make sure there were no intruders."

Chief Edwards clicked the pen and again added new data, glancing at the time. "Go home, Ian. You've done what you could. I'll keep you informed of any new developments."

"You look like you need to call it a day yourself, Reed," said Ian, noting the fatigue in the police chief's features.

"One of my officers will be here any minute. As soon as I brief him, I'm outta here." The chief's head wagged from side to side, bemused. "A southern copperhead. That's a new one for my career here in Stony Point. G'night, Ian."

Ian opened the door. "Good night." As he walked to his car, Ian resisted the urge to call Annie.

*   *   *   *

Like every normal morning during the summer, Annie spent time in her garden, weeding, watering, and gathering. Of course, the morning was not normal, but she hoped it looked so from any observer's point of view. Inside the house, Seneca was still sleeping, Boots curled up at the foot of her bed like a sentinel. All the tension of the previous few months had finally caught up with her physically, and the relief of knowing she no longer had to carry the burden alone allowed Seneca to give in to her body's demands. Even the early sunrise casting light into her room had had no effect on her sleep, as it usually did.

Annie laid a bunch of leafy greens in her harvest basket

and stood. Lifting her face to the caress of the morning, she surveyed her surroundings as though simply enjoying the beauty of the young day. However, her eyes were searching for any hints of unwanted attention. Then, tucking her gloves in a pocket of her jeans, Annie strode toward the back door, knocking the dirt from her shoes at the iron boot scrape beside the steps. As she set the basket on the kitchen counter near the sink, her cellphone rang.

Glancing at the phone, Annie saw the caller was LeeAnn. "Hi, hon!"

"Mom, I need you to be straight with me." A hint of strain hung in LeeAnn's voice, surprising Annie.

"Of course, I will be, LeeAnn." Annie had never wanted her daughter to feel like she needed to hide things from her, so she made it a habit to be as transparent with her as possible.

After a short pause LeeAnn blurted, "Is Mrs. Marchal all right?"

― 15 ―

nnie groaned inside. She was banking on the thugs needing some time to discover that Seneca had left the inn, but she knew reality favored them being on her friend's trail fairly soon. The less she talked about Seneca to others, the safer they would all be. But she didn't want to lie to her daughter. How could she keep her promise to LeeAnn to "be straight" with her now? Praying for wisdom, Annie considered her words carefully.

In the meantime, her daughter apparently realized how blunt she'd sounded. "The reason I ask is that Herb ran into Mr. Marchal this morning at a men's breakfast and just called to tell me how horrible he looked—drawn and nervous—not like himself at all. Since you'd asked me if I'd heard any news about Mrs. Marchal, I'm wondering if something has happened to her."

As soon as Charlotte had dropped Annie and Seneca at Grey Gables, Seneca had purchased the burner app to create a new phone number and had called her husband. How well Annie could understand the reason for Hunt's demeanor. Explaining that to LeeAnn was an entirely different matter.

"Hon, I will be straight with you and let you know that I can give you very little information for the time being, out of necessity. Mrs. Marchal is safe right now, and to keep her that way, we shouldn't discuss her on the phone or by email."

Annie heard LeeAnn draw in a sharp breath. "Mom, you're starting to scare me."

"I can understand why, LeeAnn. I'll tell you more as soon as I can. You'll receive a new way of contacting me before the end of the day, I promise."

"How?"

"You'll know when you receive it." Annie hated having to be so vague. She and her daughter were so used to being sounding boards for each other.

"OK, Mom, I trust you."

Relief flooded through Annie. "Thank you, LeeAnn. I love you and would appreciate your prayers for Mrs. Marchal and those of us helping her."

"You got it, Mom. I love you too. Will John and Joanna be able to talk to you later?"

Annie smiled, rubbing some moisture from her eye. "Absolutely, I want to hear how they're enjoying their summer days and what mischief they're getting into. Emily's not out of school yet, you know."

"Yes, the twins were sympathizing with her about it in their last letter, which they wrote as a cartoon series. We'll see how they feel when they're walking in the heat to school come mid-August and Em's still footloose."

Having received similar cartoon letters from her grandchildren, Annie was pleased for Emily. She knew the drawings and captions would delight Peggy's daughter, who had bonded with Joanna and John during their visits to Stony Point. "I know Em will love the letter. It'll help keep her smiling during those final school days."

"They do know how to entertain." LeeAnn's voice turned

reluctant. "I hear them stirring upstairs, and snack time is looming, so I'd better go. Mom, please be careful."

Annie knew she was right. The twins would never understand why they couldn't talk to their grandmother. "I will, hon. I'll talk to you soon. Love you."

"Back at you, Mom. Bye."

Thankfulness welled up in Annie for how calmly her daughter had received what little explanation she had been able to give. The strong-willed child had matured into a strong yet adaptable woman. How Annie looked forward to being able to have a good long conversation with her once Seneca was safe and sound. For now, Annie could only focus on taking care of her friend and supporting the efforts of Chief Edwards, Quill, and the special agent in any way she could.

She had prepared the coffeemaker for brewing, had started it up, and had washed the rhubarb and greens from the garden, spreading them out on towels to dry, before Seneca entered the kitchen. Although the strain of her ordeal was still visible on her face, her friend looked rested.

Seneca nodded at the coffeemaker. "That was thoughtful of you." She stepped closer for a good whiff of the aromatic hazelnut brew. "I don't usually drink flavored coffee, but this smells amazing."

"Alice introduced me to a coffee shop in Wiscasset that does their own roasting. I couldn't believe the difference." Annie poured a mugful and slid it across the counter to her. "We take regular road trips there for supplies. Just don't tell Peggy."

Seneca stirred a spoonful of raw sugar into her mug and grinned. "From what you've told me she probably already knows. I could use her skills at the paper."

After eating their breakfast, Annie reminded her friend about contacting Quill. "Do you have Quill's card with you?"

"I've got it." Seneca dug into her pants pocket, retrieving the card and her phone. "A. 'Quill' Quillinan. I wonder what the 'A' stands for."

"We could ask Ian when he comes for lunch," Annie said. "He might know."

Seneca sent the text to the wildlife officer and entered his phone number into her phone's address book before putting it to sleep. She looked up at Annie. "I guess now we wait."

"Let's wait with style and work on your crochet," Annie suggested, as she began to efficiently load the breakfast dishes into the dishwasher.

Seneca carried her own empty mug to the sink. "Maybe it'll help distract me from worrying about Hunt. He sounded so confused last night when I tried to explain with as few details as possible. I think I might have made it worse than if I'd simply not called at all."

Remembering what LeeAnn had told her earlier, Annie was inclined to agree with her friend's assessment, but doubted that not calling would have been the answer, either. She had already decided not to share LeeAnn's concerns with Seneca, as it would serve no purpose except to add to her friend's worries. "It was the best alternative at the time, Seneca. I'm sure Hunt will settle down once you're able to give him a little more information after you hear from the special agent."

Touching her earring and making it sway, her friend murmured, "I just hope he won't do anything rash in the meantime, like call my editor or the police demanding action or try to take matters into his own hands."

Annie nodded. "I'm sure God will give Hunt wisdom and discernment."

"You're right; I shouldn't spend time worrying about everything that could go wrong." Seneca gave her friend's arm a gentle squeeze. "Thanks."

"I'm only passing on the help from others I've received over the years." Satisfied the kitchen was in order, Annie gestured for Seneca to follow her upstairs. Her bedroom, where pleasant light poured through the closed lace curtains, seemed to her to be the best environment for their handwork and privacy. She moved to the large window to open it partway. "Here we can enjoy the fresh air without fear of being overheard. As long as we don't get too rambunctious, that is."

Seneca looked around the charming room with its antique furnishings and lovely fabrics. She had been too distracted the first time she'd been in the room to fully appreciate the details. "What a beautiful place. If we can't be laughing on the front porch, this is a good alternative. My bag is in my room, be right back." As her friend padded down the hall to the guest room, Annie retrieved her own crochet from her project bag. Boots had settled on the windowsill across from the bed, dozing in the light. Annie had briefly considered changing the curtain's color to smoky gray to better hide the inevitable collection of cat hair on the lower part of the fabric.

Seneca returned just as a pleasant breeze gently puffed billows of curtain away from the window.

"Oh, that smells and feels delightful." Seneca stepped closer to the window for more of the wind's caress.

Annie wondered if she should warn her friend to move away from the open window, but before she could decide, Seneca shook herself as if coming to her senses and stepped away. "Better enjoy the air from over here." She sat in one of the chairs angled toward each other and pulled out her crochet hook, a mini-washcloth dangling from it, and her ball of yarn. "I don't know if I'll remember what you taught me. It feels like our last lesson was years ago."

"Then we'll just have a little review before you start," suggested Annie, pulling her chair closer to Seneca's in order to instruct her friend more easily, if needed. "Soon it will feel so natural, you'll finish rows and rows automatically." Sitting down, she tucked her own supplies beside her and focused on Seneca. "First, show me what you do remember."

Seneca stared at the last row of stitches, nibbling her bottom lip and looking as though she was waiting for the yarn to speak to her. Slowly, she repositioned her grip on the hook and looped the yarn over it. At the end of the stitch, she glanced at Annie for reassurance before trying another one.

"Good," Annie encouraged her. "Just make sure you give each stitch the same amount of tension and it will be a terrific first piece. See? You remembered more than you realized."

Satisfaction dawned on Seneca's face. "I did, didn't I? You should do more teaching, my friend. Carry on Betsy's tradition."

"I have a ways to go to reach her level," said Annie. "But it's been fun sharing crochet with you, so maybe I will."

The women leaned back in their chairs, working on their individual projects. A companionable silence settled over them, and minute by minute they began to relax.

Almost entranced by the rhythmic motion, both women startled when the phone in Seneca's pocket chimed. Her hook flipped onto the rug, trailing yarn, as Seneca fumbled for the phone. Before answering, she glanced at the name and number on her phone's display. "It's Quill." Annie nodded as Seneca answered the call. "Hello?"

Seneca's eyes stared down at the handwork on the rug as she listened. Then her head lifted as she moved the phone away from her mouth and whispered to Annie, "Pen and paper!"

Annie leapt up and scoured the surface of the chest of drawers for some paper and a writing instrument, as Seneca said, "You worked fast, Quill. I appreciate it." Pulling open one of the top drawers, Annie found what she was looking for, handing them to Seneca.

"Would you spell that last name, Quill?" Seneca braced the small notepad on a leg and wrote a name and number.

"Thank you." A hint of a smile played around Seneca's mouth. "Will Mr. Geohagen be calling today?"

Seneca looked disappointed, simply responding, "Oh." She jotted something on the pad. "Quill, let me pass this on to Annie." Lowering the phone, she said, "Something will be delivered addressed to you from Ridge tomorrow. We're to look for a secret packet that will contain photos of suspected illegal animal traders and instructions."

After all the mysteries in which Annie had been involved, this was certainly a new method to her. She paused to think. "Ask Quill how will we know the delivery is from the special agent and not a ploy by the thug, if he happens to beat them to the punch. Seems like we need to be extremely cautious who we open the door for."

Seneca nodded and passed the question on to Quill. After hearing his response she relayed it to her friend, "Quill doubts the thug will try anything that involves coming to a front door in broad daylight, but said he'll text us the name of the company making the delivery."

Annie breathed out a sigh of relief. "That's helpful."

"Annie and I appreciate it, Quill," said Seneca. "I feel more hopeful this may actually be dealt with once and for all."

Seneca nodded solemnly as she listened. "There's nothing more we could ask. Bye, Quill."

As Seneca tapped the screen, ending the call, she chuckled. "Can't help but like that guy," she said. "There's something very comforting about a man who doesn't know how to schmooze. After so many years of using my powers of interpreting schmooze to hone my reporting skills, it's still refreshing when I don't have to. He did promise they wouldn't give up until they've tried every possible way of stopping the criminals."

"I agree, and I'm very relieved Quill is on our side," Annie pointed to the notepad. "So what's the special agent's name?"

Seneca gave the pad to her. Annie read the name out loud. "Ridge Geohagen. Interesting name, is that why you kind of smiled?"

"No." The small smile came back. "When I asked Quill to spell the name for me—one of the first things I learned to do as a reporter—he spelled it out so slowly and deliberately, I couldn't help but smile. I wish all the people I interview did the same."

Seneca returned the phone to her pocket and stooped to pick the yarn and crochet hook off the floor. "I'm suddenly too keyed up for more crochet right now. Do you have a mini-trampoline or exercise machine of any kind here? I don't think Quill would approve a trip to Pammy's today."

Annie snapped her fingers. "That's an excellent idea! I do have a mini-tramp. Got it before the winter weather came to stay last year. My first year here I about went stir-crazy. I went outside as much as I could, but too many days were not conducive to venturing far enough." She tucked her crochet into her project bag. "The tramp is in the den. I'll start the soup for lunch and marinate some chicken breasts. I doubt soup and salad would be enough to carry Ian through the rest of his work hours."

"Perfect." Seneca finished rewinding the yarn that had rolled out when she'd jumped at the phone call. "If I have to be under house arrest, I'm glad it's with you."

"Aw, you only say that because you like my cooking."

Seneca followed her out of the sitting room and down the hall. "There's no fooling you, Annie Dawson." She stopped before the guest room door. "I'm going to change into some looser clothes and grab my iPod. I'll be down in a minute, ready to sweat."

By the time Ian knocked on the door of Grey Gables, Seneca had jumped and bounced out some of her nervous energy. The dining room table was set for three, with a fourth chair occupied by Boots, and lunch was ready to be served.

"Something smells delicious," Ian said, as soon as he stepped into the entryway carrying a bag from the nearest mall. He reached out to give Annie a quick hug. "How's Seneca doing?"

"Seneca's doing better," the reporter called in from the dining room before appearing in person. "Thanks to Annie and her pampering."

Annie batted her eyelashes. "I try."

"Yes, you do." Ian smiled into her eyes and handed her the bag. "This isn't a typical hostess gift, but it will have to do."

Peeking into the bag, Annie nodded her satisfaction. "Today, I can't think of a gift I'd like better. Except for the dealer and his minions to be caught, of course. Lunch is ready; come sit down while I grab the chicken from the oven."

"I'll get it, Annie," said Seneca, "while you start serving the soup."

Once they were all seated and the food served, Annie and Seneca told Ian that Quill had already called.

"Excellent," said Ian. "Quill's laid back about most things, but he's always full speed ahead when it comes to his work. What's the agent's name?"

"Ridge Geohagen," Annie answered. "Do you know him?"

Ian shook his head. "He must work out of another county. He probably covers several, if not the whole state." He cut a slice from his chicken and cast a quick glance at Annie's friend before continuing. "It occurred to me last night that the break-in at Todd's shack could be connected to your ordeal, Seneca."

Seneca's eyes widened as she considered the possibility. "But that was Saturday night—the same day I arrived in

Stony Point!" Mechanically, she lowered her spoon into the soup bowl. "Were they following me all the way from Texas?"

"It may be a coincidence," Ian reminded her. "But just in case, when you talk with the agent, I suggest alerting him. The chief has probably already thought of the possibility, but I'll give him a quick call on my way back to the office."

A frown tensed Annie's face for a moment, but she didn't say anything. Then, as though shaking it off, she gave a little twitch and turned to Seneca. "You have a lot of talented people in your corner now, Seneca. No matter when he, she, or they arrived, there will not be the same amount of freedom they had when they first came."

Seneca stared down at the remaining salad on her plate as if looking for her courage there. After a moment she looked up, braving the hint of a smile. "That's true." She turned to Ian. "Thanks for not trying to shield me. We need to dig up any possible link, clue, or evidence we can."

~ 16 ~

As soon as the sun was up the next day, so were Annie and Seneca. No more sleeping late for the Southern reporter. She paced across the floor of the spacious kitchen as Annie stood before the electric griddle, making buckwheat pancakes.

"Come on, Annie, isn't there something else I can be doing? I'm really beginning to empathize with those caged animals, even more than I already did."

Annie flipped four pancakes with a deft flip of a hand. "Let's see, you set the table, replenished Boots's water and food dishes, and watered all my indoor plants. I'll wait until after breakfast before handing you the floor scrubber and bucket of suds."

The coffeemaker sputtered out the last few drops of fresh brew. Seneca's head snapped in its direction. "I'll pour the coffee!"

Annie leveled the spatula at her friend. "I'm beginning to think I should have made decaf."

"Don't even think it. Do you want to give me a headache? Then I'd be even more grouchy," Seneca warned as she filled two mugs. Sliding the tip of the spatula under a pancake, Annie lifted the bottom to see if it was ready to come off the griddle. Satisfied, she scooped it onto a plate. Seneca took a sip of the hazelnut coffee. "It's working its magic already, see?" She sat down at the wooden table, the picture of relaxation as she cradled the mug in her hands.

Slipping the last pancakes from griddle to plates, Annie set a stack in front of Seneca. "I see. Would you like home-made applesauce or 100 percent Maine maple syrup?"

"Is there a law against having both?" Seneca asked, her eyes wide and angelic.

Annie snickered and slid both jars closer to Seneca's plate. "Only if you're Boots."

After they had enjoyed their breakfast, the two friends discussed plans for the day, knowing those plans would be suspended as soon as the expected delivery occurred. Deciding to stay downstairs to make sure they could hear any arrivals at the front door, they reconvened in the library with a second cup of coffee.

"Seneca, I'm going to ask you something, and I want you to feel completely free to say no," Annie said, leaning against her grandfather's sturdy desk.

"You *do* want me to scrub the floors, don't you?" Seneca teased.

"Ha! You know, I'd forgotten about that," Annie teased back before becoming serious. "No, I was wondering if you'd be willing to share more of your research about the exotic ani-mal trade." Annie picked a paperweight off the desk, moving it from hand to hand. "I never thought about just how large an issue it is, and I'd like to know more. But I'd understand if you'd rather not talk about it any more than necessary."

Seneca leaned forward, setting an elbow on her knees and resting her chin in a hand. "It's a fascinating sub-ject, Annie. I started getting interested in it when I read a statistic from Interpol that trafficking in live wild animals is the third most lucrative illegal business in the world. Drugs and weapons bring in more, but not by much."

"Seriously?" Annie gasped. "I had no idea!"

"Absolutely, and our own dear state is quite a hotspot for it, another reason why I delved more deeply."

Annie thought about her home state for a minute and then nodded. "I'd almost forgotten. Wasn't there a to-do in McAllen when someone tried to sell some tiger cubs in a Walmart parking lot?"

"Yup. I've discovered that experts have reason to believe there are more captive tigers in Texas—just *Texas*—than there are wild ones in India. But the state only regulates the breeding of white-tailed deer!" Seneca eyed the laptop computer sitting on the desk next to Annie. "Want to try an experiment?"

"Maybe" was as much as Annie would commit herself without details. "What kind?"

"Make sure you're plugged directly into your router for security and then Google 'exotic animals for sale,'" Seneca suggested. "See what kind of links you get. Your connection is passcode protected, right?"

Annie grimaced. "It is now. Once the mysteries started popping up, I learned fast how important a lock is." She picked up her computer, plugging it into the router before sitting down in the desk chair and swiveling to face her friend. Within a minute her mouth gaped before she read aloud: "Female dromedary camel, bottle-fed." Another click. "Red kangaroo." Then, "Zedonks." She looked up at Seneca. "What are zedonks?"

"Zebra and donkey cross," said Seneca. "The zebra striping on the legs makes them quite popular."

Annie shook her head. "I'm pretty sure I've never seen one of those at a zoo." After trying another link, she gasped. "$60,000 for a baby chimp?"

Seneca nodded solemnly. "Or a Siberian tiger for $70,000. Are you beginning to see how it's such a lucrative business? And that's only a sliver of the overall live animal enterprise. Add the black market in animal body parts for traditional medicines around the world, and the scope is mind-boggling. Get this—" She paused to finish off her coffee before continuing. "I read about one of the special agents of the Fish and Wildlife Service exposing a ring of criminals who traveled around the Midwest looking for people who were frustrated with their pet tigers and offering to take them off their hands. Then they killed the tigers and sold different parts of the carcasses for a small fortune."

Shuddering, Annie stared down at her laptop and the evidence of the scary world she'd barely realized existed. A new appreciation of her friend's commitment to shining a light on the despicable "business" fanned through her. It would have been easy for Seneca to stay in the more comfortable arena of business and cultural features, and—in truth—it would have been easier for those who loved her, but Annie better understood why her friend had changed her focus to investigative reporting.

The sound of loud banging on the front door traveled down the hallway, sending both women to their feet. Annie returned the laptop to the desk, reminding

Seneca to remain hidden as she hurried to answer the knock. Pausing just long enough to peer out the front window to see a delivery van from Down East Floral Designs in the driveway, Annie pulled open the door. Quill had alerted the two women that would be the company from which the delivery would be made.

"Good morning," she greeted the woman holding a large basket arrangement.

"Hello. I have a delivery for Annie Dawson." A Maine accent permeated the woman's voice, which comforted her.

"That's me," said Annie. "How lovely!" A twinge of fear crept up her spine as she considered what could be set in motion by the contents hidden beneath the bright, delicate flowers.

The woman in a light green jacket emblazoned with the shop's logo shifted the arrangement from her arms to Annie's. "Enjoy!" The driver turned away to hurry back to the van.

Annie called out, "Thank you!" She then took herself and the basket into the hall. Placing the arrangement on an end table in the living room, she watched from the window until the van had backed out of the driveway and disappeared along Ocean Drive. Then she dashed to the library to get Seneca.

"Wow, that's something," her friend marveled at the large overflowing basket. She reached for the envelope secured by a plastic cardholder and handed it to Annie. "Since it's addressed to you, I suppose you should have the honor."

Tearing open the envelope, Annie pulled out a rectangle of heavy cardstock with a border of embossed wildflowers. In a bold script were the words, "For Annie:

Charming flowers for a charming lady! Ridge." Chuckling, she handed the card to Seneca. "Apparently, Ridge is more comfortable with schmoozing than Quill."

"So I see." Seneca put the card back into the holder and considered the arrangement. "Help me look for the photos." Both women leaned closer to examine the basket.

Annie ran a finger between the square of floral foam and the fabric liner of the basket. "It's probably either under the liner or the foam. Do you think you can lift the foam square by yourself? I'll pull out the packet, if it's there."

"Sure," Seneca said, adding with a wink, "I'll even try to not demolish the oh-so-thoughtful flowers sweet ol' Ridge sent you."

"Thank you very much," Annie primly answered, waiting for her cheeky friend to grip the large chunk of foam with both hands and slowly lift the bulky arrangement.

"It's like trying to lift a fat porcupine," Seneca muttered as a sprig of Queen Anne's lace almost poked her in the eye. "Well? Is anything there?"

Annie craned her neck, trying to see as far under the foam as possible, but she was hampered by shadow. "Hold on a second." She wedged her fingers under the square and felt around. Pulling her hand free, she shook her head. "Nothing's there."

With a "humph," Seneca lowered the arrangement back into place. "We just had to try the more difficult place first, didn't we?"

"What can I say?" said Annie. "In my experience, the more difficult place is usually where the answer is."

Seneca shrugged. "Can't argue with that, sadly." She

waved a hand at the basket. "It's your turn to do the awkward lifting."

"OK." Annie considered where to grip the liner's edges for the best leverage and grabbed as much of the fabric as she could, not wanting it to slip out of her hands. "On the count of three. One ... two ... three!" She lifted the liner free from the basket, needing to tug a little as the fabric caught on a snag along the rim of the woven basket.

"It's here!" Seneca said softly. Pulling out a manila envelope, she waved it at Annie, who gratefully lowered the liner back into its proper place.

"You know," Annie said, "somehow, when Quill told us about the photos, I didn't picture such a complicated process."

"Wait until I tell you about some of the crazy stunts animal smugglers pull to get illegal animals into the country. Talk about complicated." Seneca carried the envelope over to the couch and sat, patting the cushion next to her. "The moment of truth has arrived. Will the dealer I saw be in this photo lineup?" Annie came to sit next to her friend. "Oh, Annie. What if he's not? What if he's completely off the authorities' radars? I don't know how much longer I can hold up under this."

Annie put an arm around her friend. "One thing at a time, Seneca. But I'm sure this isn't the only trick the agent has up his sleeve. After all, you said special agents did catch those hideous people who destroyed the tigers for parts. Ridge and Quill know what they're doing, as does Chief Edwards. Isn't this much better than trying to handle it all alone?"

Pulling in a steadying breath, Seneca opened the envelope. "OK, here goes." She emptied the stack of photos onto her lap, along with a business card. Handing the card to Annie, she gave her a wavering smile. "Here's your new boyfriend's number." She lowered her eyes to the top photo. "Criminal number one, nope, not him." She flashed the scowling face in the photo toward Annie.

"Ugh, he definitely looks like someone any sane person would want to stay away from. The look in his eyes ..." Annie trailed off with a shudder.

"Next." Seneca moved the first photo to the back of the pile, revealing a new face. "This one looks like he could be an accountant! Definitely not the trafficker I saw."

Annie bent closer to the photo. "I was going to chide you for stereotyping accountants, but I must confess I did have some guys in my accounting classes at Texas A&M who could be cousins of this one."

"Sobering, isn't it?" said Seneca.

"It certainly is."

The next four photos represented different shapes, sizes, hair colors, and facial features, but none of them added up to the man Seneca had seen. But when she moved the fourth one to the back, Seneca sucked in a breath and froze.

Annie looked at the photograph and saw a face that could have been handsome if it had not been so twisted by a sneer and marred with a scar running from below one eye down to pucker the corner of his mouth. His brown hair was long and slicked back. "That's him?" she whispered.

Her friend licked her lips before answering. "Yes, I knew his mouth was shaped differently, but I couldn't see the detail of the scar." She dropped the photo into her lap as if it were poison and then began to return the entire pile to the envelope.

"Perhaps you should still look through the rest." Annie hated to suggest it, seeing how much the one face was affecting her friend. "You said there were several people there that night, right?"

Reluctance written across her face, Seneca nodded slowly. "Yes. And it's the right thing to go through all of them in case another one is there. I hate it, but you're right." Putting on her reporter demeanor, she set the photo of the one dealer on the coffee table and flipped through the rest of the pictures until she was satisfied she'd never seen any of them. "Now I can call Ridge." She pulled the phone free from her pocket, as Annie held the agent's business card out for her.

"Hello, Mr. Geohagen. This is Seneca Marchal." After a pause she responded to what the agent said. "Yes, we received the arrangement and have looked through every photo. I recognized one of them." After listening for a minute, Seneca reluctantly picked up the photo of the dealer and turned it over. "It says Ven Alaso." She held the phone out to Annie. "He wants to talk to you."

Surprised, Annie took the phone. "Yes?"

She wasn't prepared for the rich, velvet voice that spoke into her ear. "Mrs. Dawson, this is Ridge Geohagen. I need your help."

"I'm glad to do anything I can," Annie responded.

"As the person here who knows Mrs. Marchal best, I'd like to ask you some additional questions. I've set up surveillance at the inn in the room adjoining the one Mrs.

Marchal was occupying. Are you willing to come here for a short interview?"

"I am, but I'm concerned about leaving Seneca here alone," Annie freely admitted.

"I've coordinated with Chief Edwards, and he's prepared to send an officer, in plain clothes of course, to watch your home while you're gone."

Annie breathed a sigh of relief. "Then I can be there in about ten minutes."

"Thank you. Should you run into anyone you know, simply act as though you're visiting Mrs. Marchal, but go one door down the hall before knocking."

If Ridge was asking her to come to the room, they must have secured the area for the safety of the guests and it would be safe for her, as well. "I'll be sure to do that."

"Excellent," said Ridge. "The officer will be in place in about five minutes. Goodbye, Mrs. Dawson."

"I'll tell Seneca. Bye, Mr. Geohagen." She ended the call and handed the phone back to Seneca.

"He wants me to come to the inn," said Annie. "They've set up surveillance in your room."

"I figured." Seneca flipped the phone over in her hand and over again.

Annie rushed to reassure her friend. "A plainclothes officer will be here any minute to keep watch while I'm gone, and Ridge said it won't take long."

Seneca nodded and then muttered, "Ridge could have made a fortune doing radio dramas back in the day. I can't wait to see what he looks like."

"Probably very ordinary." Annie stood, understanding

her friend's attempt to distract herself. "I better get going. The sooner I leave, the sooner I'll be back."

Seneca hugged her friend. "I'll be waiting, Annie. And praying."

~ 17 ~

Connor was stationed at the main door of Maplehurst Inn when Annie arrived, greeting her with a cheerful, "Good morning, Mrs. Dawson!"

Putting aside her concern for Seneca, Annie forced a bright smile. "Nice to see you, Connor." Although she would usually stop for a brief chat with the friendly young man, this time Annie continued directly into the lobby. As she traversed the room, she noticed Linda Hunter talking to one of the desk clerks, her eyes scanning the lobby as she did so. Hoping she looked her normal self more than she felt, she started up the stairs toward her friend's former room. This time, however, she passed number 207, stopping at room 209 to rap on the door.

The man who opened the door was anything but average looking. "Mrs. Dawson?" Ridge's voice washed over her like a sultry melody.

Annie stuck her hand out between them, whether to shake the man's hand or to force him to keep a distance, she wasn't entirely sure. "Call me Annie, please." Ridge looked to be around her age, so there was no need for formality.

The special agent took her hand, enveloping her fingers briefly in his, which looked like they could play a stunning piano concerto or snap a neck with equal ease. Freeing her hand, he stepped back into the room. "Come in, Annie. And please call me Ridge."

The sound of the door closing seemed unusually loud. Ridge waved a hand toward one of the chairs flanking a round table. "Please, have a seat." The surface of the table was mostly occupied with electronic equipment that looked very unfamiliar to Annie.

"Thank you, Ridge." Annie sat down next to a monitor showing the room next door from four different angles. "Do you know the man Seneca recognized?"

Sitting opposite her, Ridge nodded. His eyes met Annie's. "Ven Alaso has been on our radar for years, but we've never been able to make anything stick. I cannot overstate how helpful Mrs. Marchal's identification will be to the ECP."

Ever since she had heard the name of the man responsible for the danger and upheaval in her friend's life, Annie's stomach had felt twisted. Somehow attaching a name to the menace made it even more real. She whispered, "Will it help keep Seneca safe? She can't keep living like this— running and being followed, threatened, and harassed." *And maybe worse things*, she thought.

Ridge reached across the table to cover Annie's hand with his. "Without going into too much of the particulars, this identification gets us much closer than we were yesterday to putting Alaso away for a long time." When Annie pulled her hand away, he gestured at the pile of equipment. "I've been monitoring Mrs. Marchal's room, in case the person who planted the snake comes back to add to his 'message.' So far, all has been quiet, and we can now begin canvasing the town for any signs of Alaso's group.

"One of the reasons I asked you to come is to make sure we have gathered every possible piece of information, either in Texas or here. The more we know, the more likely we can track down whoever followed Mrs. Marchal. I want you to feel free to share anything you think might help without fear of upsetting your friend."

"Of course," said Annie. "Although, Seneca is pretty tough, I did think of something yesterday. At first I thought I was just reading too much into it, but now I'm not sure."

Ridge unlocked a digital tablet and opened a file. "What is it?"

"Well, when we realized Todd Butler's lobster shack may have been broken into by the dealer or his thugs on Saturday night, I remembered a couple things from earlier that day. It was shortly before we first saw Seneca."

"Chief Edwards passed the information about the shack to me," said the agent. "By 'we' you mean?"

"I was with my friend, Alice MacFarlane." Annie continued. "It was late morning, and we had just begun to cross Main Street when a speeding SUV almost hit us. It had a Maine license plate, so I didn't think about it at all when Chief Edwards questioned us."

"Sometimes criminals will lift a local plate to cover their tracks," said Ridge. "I'll ask Chief Edwards to check if any have been reported as stolen. Did you notice the make of the SUV?" He inputted the information into the file.

"It was one of the large ones, a Ford, I think." Annie thought back to when she gaped at the vehicle that had almost hit her and Alice. "Black with tinted windows. Pretty much the typical crime-show cliché, now that I think about it."

Ridge flashed her an encouraging smile before asking

another question. "No bumper stickers, decals, obvious dents, or identifying marks?"

"We didn't see any on the back, but neither of us paid attention to the front. We were too busy jumping for our lives." Annie paused. "There was something else, though. Alice and I went into The Cup & Saucer diner for coffee. While we were there, a few tables of tourists arrived. As we were getting ready to leave, Alice noticed two of them who stood out because they weren't your usual tourist-type demographic, and we know most of the folks who live or work around here."

"How so?" The agent looked up from his notes. "Can you describe them?"

"I only got a quick glance because I didn't want to be too obvious about it," Annie confessed, "but they looked like they might be in their twenties, both male. One had light brown hair, maybe thinning a little on top. The other's hair was darker and more curly."

"How much darker?"

"Almost black at a glance."

"Any idea how tall they were?"

Annie thought hard, trying to picture the moment more fully. "Not really, since they were seated, but I do remember the one with lighter hair having his legs sticking out into the aisle, so I'd guess he was taller than average. The other guy might have been average or shorter, I'm not sure."

Ridge patiently asked Annie more questions until she felt he had teased every possible detail her brain had buried. She was impressed with his ability.

"This is very helpful, Annie, and I appreciate your

diligence." The agent quickly asked her a few more questions about Seneca and then told her he would use the descriptions of the two men she had given to hopefully compile a list of men who could be working for Alaso.

"Will you be able to give me photos or descriptions of the suspects?" Annie thought of Peggy and her powers of observation. "I have some friends in town who work in very public places, and I'm sure they'd like to help by keeping an eye out for them."

Considering Annie's request, Ridge paused before answering. "Quietly passing the information around could be wise. These guys flourish when citizens are too scared to do anything or don't care to get involved. If I get some matches, I can have some photos printed out for you by late today or tomorrow morning. I'll text you when they're ready for pickup."

Annie hesitated. "I wonder if my coming here combined with no more sightings of Seneca will draw unwanted notice. One of the friends I mentioned works at The Cup & Saucer and served the two men. She's also an expert observer. Since she occasionally delivers baked goods to the inn, nobody would be surprised to see her. Perhaps she could pick up the photos and bring them to us for copying, if you don't object."

"How well do you know her?" Ridge asked, his deep brown eyes searching her face for nonverbal clues.

"We've been friends ever since I moved to Stony Point," she began. "She was friends with my grandmother. She's very dependable, and she loves Stony Point."

Ridge's face lightened at Annie's description of Peggy. "Does this dependable woman have a name?"

"Peggy Carson," Annie answered. "I need to talk to her first, but I'm pretty sure she will do it."

"Fair enough. Just call me when you have her commitment. Having eyes in one of the busiest places in town could prove invaluable. These guys aren't usually the type to cook for themselves."

Annie stood, preparing to leave. "Thank you, Ridge. I better leave you to your work."

She was surprised when the agent smoothly but definitely protested. "I thought I'd show you some of the surveillance techniques we're using, so you can let Mrs. Marchal know." As curious as Annie was about the tangle of wires and such on the table, she felt nothing but the need to leave as soon as possible.

Annie replied with as firm a voice as she could muster. "As much as I would enjoy learning more about the technology y'all use, I don't feel comfortable leaving Seneca alone any longer. I hadn't planned on being away so long."

"Certainly. It's not essential," the agent recovered quickly. "I've just found reporters to be appreciative of details, just as agents are. Sometimes it reassures them." He ushered Annie to the door. "I'll keep you alerted to any progress or new information." With a final flash of perfect teeth, Ridge opened the door.

"Thank you, Ridge." Annie slipped past the man into the hall, lifting a hand for a quick wave as she walked briskly toward the stairs. She kept a wide smile on her face as she made her way through the larger gathering of inn guests and visitors, a sign that the weekend was near. A sudden longing for a rambling walk along the beach or in the woods filled her, but Annie knew that wasn't possible. Seneca needed her to be back at Grey Gables. She promised herself she'd allow plenty of time for thinking and praying come nighttime. There was too much to do before then, like contact Peggy, so Annie put all those confused thoughts and feelings on a mental shelf for safekeeping.

When Annie returned to Grey Gables, she found Seneca sitting in the living room with Boots curled in a ball beside her.

"Hmm, I see Boots is keeping you company." Annie grinned at her friend.

Seneca ran a hand along the soft fur of the cat's back. "She's a witty conversationalist for a cat. So don't keep me in suspense; sit down and tell me what happened at the inn."

Before Annie could move, they heard knocking on the front door. "Are you expecting anyone?" Seneca asked.

"No. Stay here," Annie hurried to the front door, checking through the door's peephole. When she saw Ian standing there, his military bearing as obvious as ever, she opened the door. "Hi, Ian! What a nice surprise."

Annie ushered Ian into the living room. Ian saw the large basket of flowers sitting on the table. "Wow, what an impressive arrangement!" he commented.

"It is, isn't it?" said Annie. "Feel free to read the card." She winked at Seneca.

Ian leaned closer to the arrangement. His eyes widened briefly before he laughed. "'Charming flowers for a charming lady,' huh? The agent has no idea how correct he is!"

Seneca told him, "Annie was just about to tell me how her visit with our special agent went."

Ian looked surprised. "You've already met? I hope that means good news."

"It might," said Annie. "In the basket, he sent Seneca some photos of men under investigation for illegal animal trafficking, and she recognized one of them."

Seneca jumped in, "It was the dealer himself." She looked at Annie to continue.

"His name is Ven Alaso, Ian. Apparently the agency has been investigating him for years from what Ridge told me today. You're the biggest break they've had in a while, Seneca, and they really appreciate it."

"How do you spell that?" Ian sat in a chair across from the two women and pulled out his phone to make note of it. Annie spelled both names for him.

"It's me who appreciates their help," said Seneca. "Lone Rangering is no picnic, let me tell you."

"Everyone needs their Tonto," Ian mused, glancing at Annie.

Seneca grimaced. "Well, my usual Tonto is feeling very frustrated right now. Hunt's used to being able to fix things. It's all those years in educational leadership, you know."

"I can imagine," Ian said quietly. "Annie, did the agent say what their next step is?"

Annie nodded. "He's doing surveillance on Seneca's room at the inn, in case the thug who planted the snake or anyone else tries to access it again. And he's having his assistants put together photos of anyone they know to have ever been associated with Alaso. Then he'll forward the photos and identifications to Quill and the police so they can keep an eye out around town." She paused, not knowing how Ian would react to hearing about the near miss with the SUV, but she knew he needed to know. "I also have something to tell both of you. Something I didn't connect until you brought up the lobster shack yesterday, Ian."

Annie kept the story as brief as possible, emphasizing the details of the vehicle and the men in the diner, rather than the physical danger part. Ian's eyes grew dark, but Annie continued to her point.

"Ridge is going to use the descriptions in his search, and I asked for copies of the photos of any suspects so a few of us citizens could help too."

"Which few did you have in mind, Annie?" Ian asked. "Of course, you know I'll help."

"I was thinking of the folks who would have the most opportunity to see people around town."

"Ah, that makes sense. So, Peggy, right?" Ian's eyes were serious but not challenging. "Always good to have a woman with five pairs of eyes in her head on your side."

Annie nodded, relieved. "Exactly. I do need to confirm with her, first."

Ian glanced up at the antique clock to check the time. "If you want, I can do that for you. She should be just about to get off work for today. I'll text you her answer."

Seneca spoke up. "We'd both appreciate your help with that, Ian. Annie, did Ridge give any estimate of when those photos might be ready?"

"He said either late this afternoon or tomorrow morning. Ian, could you also ask Peggy if she's willing to pick the photos up from the inn and bring them here for us?"

"I'll be sure to ask her," Ian answered. "Does Peggy have Seneca's number? She'll need it."

Seneca shook her head. "She doesn't, unless Annie gave it to her."

"I haven't had a chance yet," said Annie. "Ian, give her the new numbers for both of use, please."

"I will," Ian assured them. "People like Peggy make my job easier." He stood. "You both continue to be vigilant and keep me posted on anything new."

"We will," Annie promised, rising to see Ian to the door.

"Bye, Ian," Seneca said, bestowing a thankful smile on the mayor before he left the room.

After Annie sent him on his way with a warm kiss, she returned to the sofa.

Seneca peered at Annie's face. "Tell me more about Ridge. You only talked about his plan of action, not anything about him. What is he like?"

Annie considered answering vaguely but realized that would be foolish, so she answered honestly. "Well, I was wrong, you know. About Ridge. He isn't in the least ordinary looking. In fact, he's possibly the most handsome man I've ever met."

"I thought I detected a glimmer of something else since you came back." Seneca smiled gently.

"You know me too well, Seneca." Annie paused. "But most times, like today, I'm thankful for it. How about we go upstairs for some crochet and girl talk."

Once the two women were settled in the comfortable chairs of the sunny bedroom, Annie was ready to delve into the earlier emotions sparked by her time at Maplehurst Inn.

Annie took up her handwork with a wry grin. "Here goes. As I said downstairs, Ridge was gorgeous, and more than that, he seemed to be interested in me. And not just as a part of the smuggling case. Me."

Settling a sympathetic gaze on her friend, Seneca said, "Don't underestimate yourself, Annie. You're a smart, beautiful woman. Why wouldn't he be interested in you? The real question is are you interested in him?"

~ 18 ~

Before Annie could begin an answer, the phone in Seneca's pocket buzzed.

"Peggy has agreed to help with the photos and keep a lookout for the thugs from the diner," Seneca told her. "You know, when I go back to Texas, I'm going to feel so much better, knowing the caliber of friends you've gained here. They're pretty amazing."

"Aren't they? I've been blessed, for sure."

Seneca loosened some yarn from her cheerfully colored ball. After the additional practice, her movements were already becoming less tentative. "I'm ready for your answer now," she gently reminded her friend.

"I'm realizing most of it originates from the history of my relationship with Ian." Once she had released that admission into the air, Annie could feel something begin to unwind inside her. "Ian showed interest in me pretty much from the moment I arrived in Stony Point. But as you remember, I was nowhere ready to even consider the possibility of a new relationship after losing Wayne so unexpectedly, though it had been almost a year since it had happened."

Keeping her eyes on her handwork, Seneca nodded. "I sometimes wonder if I'd ever be able to recover enough to be open to another relationship if something happened to Hunt. It takes a lot of bravery, I think."

"I've known some women who jumped right into a new marriage, and it wasn't always a good experience for them. Sometimes, it was horrific. But my marriage with Wayne had been so strong, it took a while for me to recognize it wouldn't be unfaithful to him if I was blessed with another relationship."

Seneca looked up from her crochet, her fingers still. "Do you think Ian is that 'blessed relationship'?"

"There goes cut-to-the-chase Seneca again," said Annie, her crochet hook weaving through the thread on her hairpin fork. "That was a source of confusion for some months. First, I was simply scared and still felt like I was going to lose Wayne's memory in order to commit to Ian." She looked earnestly at Seneca. "But eventually I overcame those doubts and could admit my feelings for Ian and even act on them."

Seneca observed, "When you blush, you remind me of those gorgeous tinted photographs from the early nineteen hundreds." She wrapped her yarn around the hook. "From my perspective it's obvious Ian's totally in love with you and respects you. After spending time with both of you together, I have to say I really like him as the second love of your life." Her hook moved through another loop. "So if you've overcome the doubts, what exactly was your reaction to Ridge? Were you attracted to him?"

Annie lowered the fork into her lap and leaned forward. "Honestly, Ian holds my heart, and I'm not actually interested in Ridge, no matter how handsome he is. But remember, Ian has been the only man I've had any kind of a relationship with since Wayne died. When Ridge reacted to me the way he did, it made me wonder if I should have been more open to dating other men. Is it realistic to think I could go from one long and happy relationship right to another?"

Seneca cocked her head with a kindhearted laugh. "You mean you're thinking it's a requirement to kiss more frogs before finding your second prince?"

Annie stared at her friend, and a hand crept up to her lips. "You're right! Here I am with the gift of a wonderful relationship, and I simply can't believe it could be that easy. I have to be all in or all out, and let the Lord take care of the rest." The sparkle returned to her eyes. "I'm going to make sure Ian knows I'm in."

"OK, now stop or I'm going to start missing Hunt too much," Seneca chided with a grin.

With a happy sigh, Annie lifted the hairpin fork to resume her work only to be interrupted by the sound of her cellphone. For a moment the ring, different from the one on her new burner phone, threw her off. It seemed so long since she'd used her regular cellphone. She quickly dug to the bottom of her project bag and retrieved it. "It's Alice!" Answering the call, she said, "Alice! How are you?"

As Annie talked with her best friend, Seneca added some rows to her crochet. Annie lowered the phone long enough to silently mouth to Seneca, "Alice is flying home tomorrow."

"Oh, I'm glad! I was hoping we'd have more time together," Seneca whispered.

Then Annie's brows furrowed as she listened to Alice.

"Hold on just a minute." She muted the cellphone in case the traffickers were monitoring it, and she leaned toward her friend. "Alice's flight gets in late tomorrow afternoon. I'd like to pick her up, but the Jetport is an hour away. I'd feel better if you came with me instead of staying here alone. What do you think?"

Seneca silently considered the situation before speaking. "By then we'll already have the photos from Ridge, so that won't be an issue. I can stay crouched low until we're out of town. If we're careful about getting me into the car, I don't see why I can't go with you. Do you think we should run it by Chief Edwards?"

"You're right." Annie returned the phone into position. "OK, Alice, I've worked it out. I'll be there; I can't wait to see you." Clicking the phone off, she tucked it into her jeans' pocket, rather than returning it to her project bag. "I don't know about you, but I'm feeling much better than I did an hour ago."

"I'll chime in with a big amen," said Seneca. "After all, I actually get to leave the house for a couple hours tomorrow. Now I'm so excited I can hardly sit still!"

"Sounds like it might be a good mini-tramp time. We'll have plenty of time for more crochet tonight."

Seneca sprang from her chair. "Yes, it does! But what are you going to do?"

"I think I'm going to plan a little welcome-home surprise for Alice." Annie rubbed her hands together, the wheels already turning.

By the time Seneca received a text from Ridge, she had already exercised, showered, and changed. Evening was fast approaching. She hurried into the kitchen where Annie was baking for Alice's return. "Hey, Ridge says the photos are ready for pickup. Do you think Peggy has left the diner yet?"

"I'm not sure," Annie answered, opening the oven to slide a large Bundt pan inside. "I'll just have to try her cellphone. At least it's too late for the supper rush, which is definitely not a good time to interrupt her."

Annie's call caught Peggy just as she had finished her shift and was about to leave for home. Her friend immediately promised to stop by the inn and Grey Gables before going home. Shaking her head, Annie clicked off the burner cellphone. "That girl! She's so excited. I'm not sure if it's because she's helping an actual special agent or because we've asked her to do undercover snooping of unfamiliar customers. I hope this doesn't have adverse effects on Stony Point tourism."

Seneca chuckled. "Aren't eccentric characters supposed to be a plus for tourism?" She looked around at the baking clutter. "Why don't you let me clean this up? It'll be my contribution to Alice's homecoming surprise, and you can make the photocopies for Peggy after she arrives."

A couple hours later the two women climbed the stairs to the second floor, satisfied with the day's work and ready for a night's rest. Peggy's enthusiasm and Ridge's efficient professionalism had given both women a reason to be optimistic.

The next day, after Annie finished her gardening, and she and Seneca enjoyed breakfast, she asked her friend if she had any preferences on how they should spend their time before leaving for the Portland Jetport. They had already looked through the photos of possible accomplices of Alaso, and while Annie was disappointed, she didn't see any men who looked obviously like the two men in the diner, but she remained hopeful. Seneca told Annie she had something else in mind. She wanted to experience the magic of the notorious attic.

"You're more likely to experience dust than magic," Annie teased. "But I happen to know you've been in worse places, so why not?" She wagged a finger at her friend. "Just be warned, I have no intention of starting any new mysteries. We've already got enough to tackle."

Seneca put her hands up in surrender. "I've had more than enough adventure for the month, have no fear. I just love seeing old stuff, as you well know."

After Seneca helped Annie put together a slow cooker dinner for later, the women went up the stairs to the second floor and down the hall to the door at the bottom of the attic steps. Before opening the door, Annie told Seneca, "No matter how often I try to keep this place tidy, it always seems to be dusty. We'd better make sure we don't lose track of time because we'll definitely need to shower before we leave for Portland."

"Gotcha." Seneca eyed the old-fashioned knob on the door. "I love how your grandparents kept so many of the original features of the house."

Annie opened the door and waved for her friend to go first. "It wasn't until I inherited Grey Gables that I realized how much work Gram and Grandpa must have put into its upkeep and preservation all those years. It almost wore me out the first year, catching up with some needed repairs after the years of Gram's declining energy."

At the top of the stairs Seneca stopped short. "Wow! It's even better than I'd imagined. What a marvelous place!" Sunlight poured in through the window that was set into the wall opposite them, casting a wide spotlight on the piles of curiosities. "No wonder you have so many fond memories of playing up here."

Annie picked her way through the miscellany. "What amazed me after being away so many years, is how I remembered some of these very things from childhood but also how I kept finding more unfamiliar and mysterious items. That's one of the reasons I was so excited to allow John and Joanna to play up here when they visited—after making it less hazardous!" She paused before a dress form, pulled a dust-cover up far enough to reveal a sweeping emerald green dress embellished with gold embroidery. "So the memories continue to another generation. I used to dress up in this gown when I visited my grandparents during the summers when I was young. Last Thanksgiving Joanna wore it for the first time." She ran a loving finger along the intricate embroidery. "You know, it was a magical memory for me, now that you mention the 'magic' of the attic." Her face grew as still as the old dress form.

As the silence lengthened, Seneca touched her friend on the arm. "You're looking pensive, Annie."

Annie shook herself out of her memories. "I was just thinking how important creating those moments with John and Joanna has become to me. LeeAnn didn't get a chance to have those with her grandmother, and I've always felt sad for her." Annie had long ago come to a place of peace about the timing of her parents' deaths, as well as their career in missions which had often kept them separated from her during her own childhood. But those hard things still created ripples in her life and that of her daughter.

Seneca picked up a dented metal enameled pitcher, wiping the dust off to better see the color and pattern underneath. "Don't think your effort is lost on LeeAnn. I ran into her after their visit last year, and she raved about the wonderful time the twins had with you here." She held the pitcher out at arm's length. "I would use this for autumn flowers on the porch steps, alongside some pumpkins and gourds. And the pumpkins wouldn't rot after only two hours outside, either!"

Taking the vessel from Seneca, Annie considered her suggestion. "You're right, it would look quirky and homey." She cast her eyes around the attic. "We could probably find enough different kinds of containers to completely fill the porch!"

"With a sign at the bottom of the driveway that reads: 'Warning! Dangerous quirk overkill ahead!'" Seneca moved deeper into the attic's expanse. "This is so much fun. Mind if I poke inside cabinets, drawers, and such?"

Annie returned the pitcher to its original place. "Poke away. Just remember, if you find a new mystery, you're going to have to solve it yourself."

"That's a risk I'm willing to take." To emphasize her answer, Seneca carefully slid open the wide but shallow drawer of a battered table. Drawing in a short breath of discovery, she drew out an old fountain pen from the drawer. "This is beautiful! They don't make pens like this anymore." Laying the amber pen reverently on her palm, she carried it to Annie. "Look at the craftsmanship! I bet with a little clean-up it would still work great."

Annie bent for a closer look at the pen. "Is the cap screwed on?"

Seneca gently twisted the cap. "Yes!" Lifting it off, they saw the name "Parker" etched on the nib with the words "Lucky Curve Pen" underneath. "Annie, this is a Bakelite jack-knife pen! It must be a hundred years old!"

Annie loved her friend's enthusiasm. "Why don't you take it as a memento of the attic? It's a waste to have it stuck up here when you see its beauty."

Her friend clasped the pen closer and then pulled it away to check for staining. "Oh, Annie, really? Thank you! Once all this trafficking nonsense is ended, I'll display it proudly in my office at the paper." A sly look skirted over her face like a cheeky cloud. "Or somewhere else."

"Somewhere else?" Annie jumped on the phrase immediately. "Is there another surprise up your sleeve, my friend? Are you leaving the *Star* soon? Don't tell me you and Hunt are thinking of moving."

Seneca slipped the pen between her thumb and forefinger, testing its balance. "Bite your tongue, Annie Dawson! You know we'd never do that." She looped invisible words through the attic air. "The newspaper business has been changing for years—a light-speed kind of change. I'm thinking about branching into a different direction."

Annie wondered if the scare of her present predicament

was the spark for this possible career switch, more than the changes in the business of which she spoke. "Different atmosphere? Are you thinking of going back to school?"

"Oh, no!" Seneca exclaimed. "Nothing like that. I'm too ornery for the classroom, you know." She peered back into the drawer, running a hand along the bottom. She muttered, "Hmmm, I was hoping the box would be in here somewhere." Straightening back up, she looked Annie in the eye. "I'm simply thinking, seriously, of going freelance and working from home. Maybe even write a book."

Rummaging through a pile of small things gathered in a cracked pottery bowl on top of the table, Annie thought about this new revelation from Seneca. "You certainly have the discipline for it," she encouraged her friend. "So— would you write a book about your forays into the seedier side of commerce?"

"I think I'll wait to see how this particular story ends first." Seneca cast an eye at the bowl. "See anything that looks like a fountain pen box?"

Annie shook her head. "Nope. It might be up here somewhere, but it would probably be quicker to carve our own box. We have plenty of time to look some more, though."

The women lingered, exploring the attic and discussing some of the ideas Seneca had gathered for independent writing projects. In spite of their initial awareness of when they needed to leave for Portland, time still got away from them. By the time Annie thought to check her phone for the time, they had not allowed much of a buffer to make themselves presentable, particularly Annie, since they had no intention of presenting Seneca to anyone except Alice.

Annie warned her friend of their need to hurry, and they both clattered down the stairs, bent on not keeping Alice waiting for her ride home.

~ 19 ~

An hour later, Annie maneuvered her Malibu through the Jetport traffic to the "cellphone lot," a parking area reserved for motorists picking up arriving passengers. Once she had found a free spot, she parked and eyed the car's clock before turning off the engine. "Whew! We made it. Unless the plane ran into some unexpected delays, Alice is probably getting her luggage right about now." She dug her phone from her purse to alert her friend that they had arrived and where they were parked.

"This is the first time I've ever greeted a traveler while lying down in the backseat," mused Seneca. "At least you didn't make me ride in the trunk."

Annie finished her text and sent it. Snapping the phone closed, she forced herself to not look over her headrest to address Seneca. "It might have been more foolproof if we had." Her eyes darted to a car entering the parking lot. Following it as it slowly drove past them, Annie looked for details while trying to appear nonchalant. She relaxed as a woman and a teenager exited the car, hurrying toward the baggage claim side of the airport.

Alice's reply text arrived. "She has her luggage and is on her way out!" Annie exited the car, but stayed next to it, ready to wave to Alice as soon as she spotted her. A low rumbling alerted her that a rolling suitcase was heading in their direction, and Alice's tired face soon appeared around a corner. "Alice!"

As weary as she looked, Alice's stride quickened when she saw Annie waving. Annie wondered if she had been able to sleep at all during her time in Florida. It appeared doubtful. She opened the trunk and met Alice to take her suitcase.

Alice opened her arms to embrace her friend before handing over her luggage. "You are a sight for sore eyes, Annie Dawson. Remind me to never go to Florida in June ever again. How did you stand it in the South?"

"I'm so glad you're back!" Annie exclaimed. "How was the flight?" She hefted the bulky bag into the deep trunk.

"Once we got into the air, it was fine. But we sat on the tarmac for too long before taking off, and it got uncomfortably hot, fast." She lifted her face, as if pressing against the cooler Maine air. "We all cheered once we finally took off."

"They must have made up some time in the air," Annie observed. "Your plane arrived right on time." She unlocked Alice's door for her before returning to hers. "You can nap on the way home, if you'd like."

Alice slid into her seat before shaking her head. "No way. I want to hear what you've been up to while I was gone." She craned her neck over the seat, startled to see Annie's friend lying sideways in the back. "Hi, Seneca. Are you having back problems?" she asked, concern in her voice.

"Hi, Alice. Um, no back problems, thanks," came Seneca's answer.

Alice's eyes hovered between the backseat and Annie. "Why do I get the feeling you two have had a week as eventful as mine?" She settled back against the padded seat. "Do tell."

"Could we hear about your mother's memorial service, first?" Annie asked as she edged out of the parking space. "Was it a comfort to you?"

Alice stared out the window. "The service itself was. I hadn't realized how many people Mother had in her life down there. The memorial was well attended, and it was encouraging to hear about the different ways Mother had settled into the community during the luncheon afterward." She turned toward Annie, adding, "The preparations were more difficult. I'm still processing it all in my mind, so maybe now would be a good time to hear about what's been happening in Stony Point while I was gone."

Respecting Alice's wishes, for the rest of the ride Annie and Seneca took turns explaining the twists, turns, and frights they had been navigating and the current state of the investigation. "There's even a possibility the SUV that almost mowed us down could have been involved."

As Annie turned onto Main Street, heading for Maple, Alice shook her head in amazement. "I simply cannot leave you for any length of time, Annie Dawson, without you finding one conundrum or another to plunge into."

"To be fair," Seneca interposed, "this time the conundrum found her. I did feel guilty at first, as soon as I realized the traffickers had found me even in tiny Stony Point, but I have to admit, I've also been relieved to not be handling it alone anymore."

Alice peered over the backseat before remembering they were now in Stony Point, and it was imperative that it seem like only she and Annie rode in the Malibu. Cocking her head to the opposite direction, as though she was simply relieving neck tension, she admitted, "You're right, I do have to credit you with that. But, as you said, it's better to not be tackling this alone, so I'm glad you fled here, Seneca. I'd like to help too."

Annie could tell from the silent backseat that her friend was moved by Alice's offer. She had turned into the driveway leading to Alice's cottage before Seneca's response came. "Your offer means a lot to me, Alice. But first, you need to unpack and rest."

The sound of a grumbling stomach echoed from the passenger side of the car. "And scavenge some grub," added Alice, scowling at her midsection.

"Oh *please*," Annie teased. "Did you really think we'd let you come home to no dinner? I'm insulted. As soon as you've unpacked and done whatever else you need to do, come to Grey Gables for dinner." She turned off the engine and exited to open up the trunk.

Alice met her from the other side, relief written on her face. "Thank you, thank you! I'll be over as soon as I've washed the Florida humidity off from head to toe." Reaching into the trunk, she lifted the suitcase and set it down to extend the handle. She paused to take in her familiar surroundings and then sighed. "It's good to be home."

After she watched Alice unlock her front door and enter the cottage, Annie returned to the driver's seat. Backing out of the driveway, she immediately turned into her own, keeping her eyes roving over the area for any signs of unwanted visitors. When all seemed quiet, she pulled up to Grey Gables. But her breathing was shallow until she and Seneca were securely ensconced in her cheerful kitchen, where the chicken and vegetables bubbled, and Boots sat munching a snack from her bowl.

While Annie added peas to the slow cooker and mixed together the dumpling batter, Seneca retrieved the table decoration they had made the day before to celebrate Alice's return. By the time Alice knocked on the door, the dumplings were fluffy and floating on top of the chicken and dumplings. Sweet tea with mint fresh from Annie's garden sat on the table. The chocolate Bundt cake was hidden away in a cabinet.

Alice entered the kitchen, stopping in her tracks when she noticed the large decoration declaring "Welcome Home, Alice!" in letters drawn to look like cross-stitch. When Alice looked like she might burst into tears, Annie began to realize just how much of a toll Alice's trip had taken on her. "Take a seat, any seat," she told Alice, trying to keep the atmosphere light.

Throughout the meal and dessert, the three women talked of many things, both light and weighty, often letting Alice steer the conversation. As they sat with their hunger satisfied, Alice asked again how she could help with the investigation of the men who were threatening Seneca. Annie brought the photos Ridge had developed for them and showed them to Alice. "When you're in town, would you keep a look out for any of these men?" Seneca asked her. "If you see one or more, we don't want you to confront them, but alert Annie or Ian or me, and we'll contact the agent. We don't want them to be able to connect you to the investigation."

"This shouldn't be too hard. I'm pretty good with

faces." Alice sifted through the photos, using her creative abilities to notice distinguishing characteristics of each face and store them in her memory. Stopping at one photo, she squinted at it more closely. "Hmmm, if you change this guy's bleached long hair and replace it with a shorter, thinning brown variety, he could possibly be one of those guys in the diner."

"Really?" Annie held her hand out for the photo. When Alice released it to her, she took a good long look. "You're good! I completely skipped over him. I'll text Ridge and Chief Edwards, and let them know." She pulled out her burner phone and sent them the new information.

As she watched Annie, a yawn caught Alice by surprise. She clapped a hand over her mouth. "Man, my body keeps betraying me today."

"Alice, why don't you stay with us tonight?" asked Annie as she closed the phone. "We promise to let you sleep as long as you want tomorrow."

Seneca added, "Like Annie always says, there's plenty of room, and I promise not to hog the guest bath."

A tired smile crossed Alice's lips. "How can I say no to such hospitality?" Her eyes moved to the decadent cake sitting in the middle of the table. "Hmmm, cake for breakfast has a nice ring to it too. You've convinced me." She stifled another yawn. "I'm afraid someone might have to help me up the stairs, though."

Annie patted her friend's hand. "Just rest a minute while we put away the food, and we'll all settle in for the night. It's been a long day for all of us."

Alice pushed her dinner dishes to the side and lowered her head onto her folded arms. Seneca and Annie made quick work of the dinner cleanup and then roused their sleepy friend. "Here we go, Alice. Your reward for climbing the stairs is that you get to sleep in my old room," Annie informed her. "But I'm sure you won't be awake all night giggling with me like we used to do."

"Maybe tomorrow," Alice joked, groggy with fatigue. Once they arrived at the bedroom, Alice looked down at her shirt and jeans. "Why did I have to wear jeans?"

"Don't worry, I have plenty of extra nightclothes," Annie told her before ducking into her room for an extra pair of comfortable pajamas. Once her friends were tucked away in their rooms, she completed her own nighttime routine and climbed under the light summer quilt on her bed with Boots curled at her feet. She had opened the windows to invite the fresh night air inside and luxuriated in the sensation, letting it lull her to sleep.

Something thumped above her head. Then, *th-thump*. Annie knew Grey Gables by now—all its idiosyncrasies and settling noises. This didn't belong in either of those categories. Trying to squelch the panic before it took over her, Annie considered what might have made the noise. The eyebrow windows on either end of the attic did not open. They had been put there for light, not circulation. The larger window opposite the door had been closed when she and Seneca had been up there earlier in the day. Annie rarely opened the window, as she dreaded it being left open during one of the heavy storms that blew up so fast on the coast.

The weight of Boots's lithe body rested over her foot, negating that possibility. Maybe one of them had left something leaning too close to a table edge and gravity had just won.

A different kind of clatter sent Annie to an upright position, her mouth suddenly dry. In a moment she was out of the bed, sliding her feet into the slippers by her bed and creeping out into the hallway. A shadow moved, drawing a gasp from her that she tried to muffle by clapping a hand over her mouth.

"Annie, it's me!" Alice hissed near her ear. "But what is *that?*" She jerked a thumb up toward the attic. "Did Boots get up there?"

Annie shook her head, pointing over her shoulder at her bedroom door. "She's on my bed. Let me get my flashlight." On tiptoes she scurried into her room, grabbing the light from her bedside table.

When she returned to the hallway, Seneca emerged from her room. "What's up?"

Alice gestured above them. "There might be someone— or something—in the attic. Didn't you hear the noises?"

"Yes, but I haven't been here long enough to know what noises are normal for Grey Gables," Seneca explained.

"Grey Gables makes gentle sighs and sounds," whispered Annie, "not thumps and clatters."

Seneca's eyes grew wide and flitted upward. "What should we do? I can call the police." She lowered her eyes toward Annie.

"Not yet. It might just be a squirrel or chipmunk." Annie thought of her little visitor in the yard, although she knew full well the light creature could not be making the sounds they were hearing.

Alice raised an eyebrow but kept quiet before whispering, "Do you have anything we can use for defense, just in case?" Seneca put up a hand and slipped back into her room. A moment later she returned with two things, a dagger-like letter opener and a sturdy walking stick.

She shrugged her shoulders. "They might help in a pinch, anyway."

Annie pointed at the walking stick. "I'll go first with that." Seneca held it out, and she grasped it firmly in the middle. Taking a deep breath, Annie whispered, "Let's go." She crept toward the attic door, with Seneca and finally Alice following. When she reached out for the knob, she was surprised to see the door sagging open. Grimacing as she realized she had probably not closed the door securely earlier, she nudged the door wider and began to cautiously climb the steps.

As she crested the top of the steps, Annie reached for the light switch. When she did not immediately find the switch, she turned on her flashlight—and shrieked as wide green-gold eyes reflected in the beam of light. She flung out a hand once more in an attempt to find the light switch, and this time the overhead lights flooded the room. A rumbling growl bounced off the walls, sending Annie stumbling back onto her friends' feet. "Get out!" she yelled, flourishing the walking stick and flashlight in front of her at the giant spotted cat, as she fought to not fall on the way back to the attic door.

Alice and Seneca sprang for the door, dragging Annie

with them. They tumbled into the hallway, Annie slamming the door behind her. She slumped against the solid wood door, sucking in air.

"I think it's safe to assume Alaso's friends came for a visit while we were out!"

~ 20 ~

*H*er legs trembling, Seneca pushed her dark hair away from her face. "I'll call Ridge and Quill." She looked down at the letter opener still in her hand, as she walked to her room. Turning back to Annie, she asked, "What *was* that, anyway?"

Annie was still slumped against the door, as if to keep the animal from breaking out of the attic. "A leopard, I think. I saw spots—and this time it wasn't my eyes going bad." She couldn't hold back a shudder.

Seneca stared at the attic door behind Annie before disappearing into her room. A moment later she returned to the hallway, phone in hand. She keyed in the numbers and then held the phone to her ear. After a few seconds, Ridge answered, and Seneca filled him in on the horror they had just experienced. After a brief consultation, she closed the phone. "He'll be here in ten minutes." She checked the time on her phone's display. "This might sound crazy, but I'm sure glad we turned in early so we didn't have to call him after midnight."

Alice mustered a wry chuckle. "This isn't early for Annie. This is well past her bedtime." She gestured at Seneca's phone. "Did … his name is Ridge, right? Did Ridge have any instructions for us? Other people to call?"

"Not yet," Seneca answered. "I don't even have to call

Quill. Ridge is calling him in to help too, but he said he'd prefer to keep it quiet for now. He also said he would let Chief Edwards know what is going on, but he doesn't want uniforms on the scene at this point."

"I feel much better knowing Quill's coming also," said Annie.

Alice nodded. "Quill, eh? He's one tough hombre. Only person I know to take on a moose and get away with it." She shook her head at the memory of the incident. "A couple of people could have gotten seriously hurt, if he hadn't been nearby. If anyone can handle that ... leopard—it's Quill."

"He was pretty efficient with the copperhead, as well," added Seneca. "*Blech.*"

Alice looked down at her borrowed pajamas. "Hey, Ridge will be here soon. Why don't you two get into some street clothes?" She looked at Annie, still pressed against the attic door. "I'll take your post at the door, though I doubt we can hold him if he seriously wants out."

"Well, he hasn't tried to get at the door yet," said Annie. "That old lock does have a key, although I don't know how sturdy it is after all these years. I'll grab it after I change." She stepped away from the door, but paused at the door of her bedroom until she was sure Alice had taken her place.

Seneca waited with Alice until Annie returned in a light tunic and soft capris, a skeleton key in hand, before slipping into her room. Before she returned, a screaming roar speared through the night. Even though Annie had already locked the attic door, color drained from both Annie's and Alice's faces as they sat with their backs against the only thing between them and what now sounded like a very angry carnivore.

As Seneca tumbled out of her room, one shoe still in her hand, there came another terrifying sound. The sound of shattering glass. A large amount of glass.

"That was no vase breaking," stammered Annie. "That was the big window."

Hopping on one foot, Seneca quickly put on her other shoe and then hurried into the sitting room to look out of the large window. "It's in the big tree!"

"She must mean the sugar maple," said Alice. "Now what do we do?"

Annie winced, not sure, until she considered how fast leopards could run and the small size of the town. "I think we have to call 911 now. We have no way of knowing if the leopard's going to stay here until Ridge and Quill get here." She called for Seneca to bring her the burner phone from where she had left it earlier. She quickly called 911.

"This is Annie Dawson at 1 Ocean Drive, Stony Point. There is a large cat in one of my sugar maples." Before she could explain further, she was interrupted. After listening she continued. "No, I don't think it can wait until morning. The big cat is a leopard, a spotted leopard to be exact. Ridge Geohagen and Quill Quillinan are already on their way, but when it jumped out of my attic and into the tree, I thought it best to call you, in case the leopard leaves my yard before they arrive."

A moment later, Annie closed the burner phone, shaking her head. "Congratulations, Alice. You're not friends with a crazy cat lady; you're friends with a crazy woman who had a leopard in her attic."

"Spotted leopard," Alice added. "You can't leave out that little detail."

Annie gasped. "Ridge and Quill need to know before they arrive. Seneca!" she called to her friend who had just returned to the window and was watching the leopard in the tree.

"What?" Seneca poked her head out of the bedroom.

"Text or call Ridge and let him know where the leopard is now."

"Oh!" Seneca clapped a hand to her temple. "You're right!" She stepped back into the room, pulling out her phone.

Alice turned to Annie as they still sat with their backs against the door. "We can leave our post now, don't you think? We'll have to open the door for the guys, anyway."

"They're not going to let us do that until they've tranquilized and caged the leopard, I'm sure." Annie wrinkled her nose. "And I'm OK with that." Realizing Alice was still dressed in pajamas, she suggested her friend change back into her jeans.

A few minutes later, after Alice had returned from Annie's childhood room, Seneca called from the sitting room, "They're here!" Annie and Alice joined her at the window, watching as the truck drove slowly up the driveway without lights. Both Ridge and Quill jumped out and moved to the bed of the truck to retrieve a very large cage. Ridge reached back into the cab, withdrawing a large rifle.

Annie gasped. "Please tell me that's a tranquilizer gun."

"It is," Seneca assured her. "I saw some when I was

interviewing animal conservation people in Texas." Her eyes moved back to the maple tree. She tugged at her bottom lip with her teeth. "It looks like the leopard's getting antsy. He probably smells the guys."

The three women remained glued to the window, peering from tree to the men and back to the tree, as they watched the capture attempt unfold. Ridge and Quill carried the cage between them, using gliding steps that reminded Annie of the drum majors at football games. But they knew better than to try to get the cage too close.

In spite of their efforts, the leopard became more agitated, moving from branch to branch, pacing in the tree.

"I can't stand it anymore," Annie gasped. "I'm going downstairs."

Seneca turned to her. "Don't you dare go outside, Annie!"

"I won't until it's safe," Annie promised as she hurried toward the stairs.

"Wait! I'm coming too," Alice called. Annie paused to let her catch up. They descended the stairs side by side and ran to look out of the dining room window. A moment later they saw a blur as the leopard launched itself from a branch of the tree, clearly hit by a dart.

The graceful cat crumbled onto the grass. Footsteps pounded down the stairs, and Seneca rounded the banister to join them. "Did you see that?" she yelled. "What a shot!"

Annie stared at the leopard through the glass. "Are you sure it's OK? It looks horrible—so still."

"Don't you think it's safe enough for us to go out there now?" Alice asked. "Except maybe Seneca, since they still haven't found any of the traffickers."

Seneca gave a little growl of frustration. "I know. I don't like it, but I know. You two go out there and get the details for me, will you?"

Alice shot her a look of respect, and then nodded. "We can do that, right, Annie?"

"I don't know," Annie said. "Tranquilizers can sometimes take awhile before they take full effect. Let's wait to get some sign from Quill and Ridge."

Ridge and Quill carefully approached the leopard, Quill checking its vital signs. Watching him go through the steps, Annie was reminded of her grandfather and his gentle way with animals. She leaned against Alice in relief when she saw him nod to Ridge, and they both bent to move the sleeping leopard.

The men then paused and motioned that it was safe for the women to come outside the house. Annie squeezed Seneca's hand before leaving her at the window to go outside onto the porch with Alice. The quiet of the night seemed unearthly after the tension of their last hour. The two friends stole across the porch to get closer to the majestic animal that had caused them so much terror.

"I'll kill you!" A snarling yell hurled through the quiet of the yard. "If that cat is dead, you are dead!" Alice leaned over the railing of the porch, looking in the direction of the path down to the beach met Annie's yard. The threatening voice was definitely approaching the house from the pathway.

Both Annie and Alice yelped when they realized the very angry man was fighting to release himself from Ian Butler's military-trained grip. Alice grabbed Annie's arm and whispered, "Listen! Sirens!"

"Hold onto him, Ian!" Annie whispered, mostly to herself, not wanting to distract any of the men who were there to protect them. Ian had several inches on the man, but she'd never seen anyone buck and twist like that.

With efficient moves born of years of practice, Quill and Ridge secured the leopard in the cage and turned to assist Ian. The stocky man refused to be cowed, even at being suddenly outnumbered. "If that cat is dead, my boss will be out for blood." He snarled up at Ian's face, "Yours!"

Ian had trained his face to stay calm and his grip tight. Ridge checked the thug for weapons, pulling a small handgun from under his pants leg. He nodded at Ian. "Impressive. You got to him before he could pull this."

"He was talking on the phone when we heard the cat scream and fall," Ian explained, as he changed his grip to position the man between himself and Quill. "I jumped him when he ran past me." He jerked his head back toward the beach path. "He dropped the phone when I tackled him. From what I heard, I'd say he was talking to his boss."

A police car turned into the driveway, stopping behind Ridge's truck. Reed Edwards's long powerful frame unfolded from the inside of the car and strode toward the three men. "Evening, Mayor. Who've you got there?" He eyed the still struggling man.

Ridge held out the handgun. "The carrier of this concealed weapon, for starters. Now that you're here, Reed, I can go bag the phone he dropped. This one's just the tip of a very dark iceberg."

"Since I received the emergency call about a leopard that found its way, *somehow*—" Ridge glared at the captured man, "—into the attic of Mrs. Dawson's house, I picked up Quill. When Quill and I arrived, the cat had broken through the attic window and was in that tree." He pointed out the sugar maple where the leopard had been. "We tranquilized the cat, and it's sleeping it off in a cage." He pointed a thumb to the back of his truck.

Reed nodded. "OK, go get the phone before we go any further." Ridge jogged toward the beach path and disappeared down the slope.

Alice turned to whisper in Annie's ear. "What if they can't find enough evidence to keep the thug in jail? Seneca will still be in danger."

"I think they can start with the concealed weapon charge and go from there," Annie guessed. "Ridge has been investigating Alaso for a long time. I'm hoping he's got stuff that they can try to connect to the thug." She remembered what the man had shouted at Ian. "I don't know, but maybe they can add something for the threats against Ian, him being a public official."

The hint of a grin crept onto Alice's face. "I sure would have liked to see Ian tackle that guy." She peered across the yard.

"He had a gun, Alice!" Annie clinched her teeth. The reality of the situation began to more fully dawn on her. *What was Ian doing there?* "Ian could have been killed."

Alice put an arm around her friend. "But he wasn't, Annie."

Annie nodded and then pointed toward the beach path from where Ridge had just returned. "Looks like he found it!" The agent swung a plastic evidence bag, his gait showed a hint of swagger.

The men conferred quietly, frustrating the women who were trying to listen from the porch. They could, however, see the angry man lose some of his fire and hoped it was a sign of good things to come. After some minutes of discussion, Ridge and Chief Edwards escorted the cuffed trafficker to the police car, and Quill returned to the truck to check on the leopard. Ian approached the porch.

"Ian!" Annie rushed down the steps, flinging her arms around him. She hugged him hard, and then stepped back and punched him on the arm. "What were you doing? You scared me!"

Ian pulled her back into his embrace, running a hand over her hair. "I know, Annie. I'm sorry, but I had to protect you, no matter what."

"How did you find him?" she asked, her face pressed against his shoulder.

Noticing Alice behind Annie, looking both amused and a little uncomfortable, Ian stepped back, took Annie's hand and led her to the door. "Let's all go inside for a minute so Seneca can hear too. Then I need to go with Quill. We're going to the police station for official statements. Reed will call on you and Seneca for your statements tomorrow."

Seneca greeted them as soon as they entered the foyer. "It's about time! What is going on?" They gathered in the living room to hear Ian's story.

"I knew Ridge and Quill were doing what they could to crack the case and protect Seneca from Alaso," he began, "but I still wasn't comfortable with you ladies being here alone. So I started spending my unscheduled time keeping a watch on Grey Gables, in case I saw any signs that the thugs had located Seneca again."

"Well, give the man some armor and dub him a knight!" exclaimed Alice. "Guess someone had to, since I was gone."

"You're irreplaceable, Alice," said Ian, "but I tried. I even skulked around the back of your cottage a few times, to check out that side of the property."

"I can't believe I never saw you!" Annie was clearly amazed at Ian's actions.

He brushed a lock of hair from her brow. "It wasn't always easy to stay hidden. Do you know how fetching you are when you garden early in the morning?"

They gazed at each other until Alice reached over Annie to smack Ian on the knee. "There are other people here! Go on!"

A sheepish grin captured his face, and he continued. "Each day I checked the beach path for signs of use, footprints, or debris—dressed in old beachcombing clothes, of course. I realized it would be a simple way of accessing the house with a better chance of not being seen, so I stationed myself behind a rock to listen for while. Then I heard someone talking as he came up the path. After listening, I realized the guy was probably talking to Alaso." He looked at Seneca, who clutched her hands together.

"When he heard the sound of breaking glass, the guy charged up the path toward the house. I jumped him as he passed me. I didn't know what his intentions were, but I knew they couldn't be good."

"That must have been some tackle, to make the guy drop his phone," Alice mused.

"You can thank Todd for that." Ian laughed. "We spent a

lot of time wrestling and tackling each other as kids. Guess we watched more *Pink Panther* movies than we should have."

Seneca snorted. "I'd say you watched just the right amount. Now, maybe the police and Ridge can convince the thug to give up Alaso." A faraway look came to her eyes. "And I might actually make it home soon." She smiled at Alice. "As hot as it is, it's still home."

~ 21 ~

"It surely is nice to enjoy the cozy atmosphere of Stony Point again," said Seneca, as she, Annie, and Alice strolled down Main Street to A Stitch in Time. "Finally—no fear."

"I'm going to miss you," Annie told her. "We need to make sure we Skype more often, so I can hear all about your new writing career."

Alice added, "Mind if I join Annie sometimes? It would be nice to get to know you more without the distractions of big cats and guns."

"I'd like that, Alice." Seneca strode ahead of the others to open the door of the shop. "Now, y'all help me pick out some more yarn for the ride home. I plan to let Hunt do all the driving, this time." She grinned as her friends entered the shop before her. "I can't believe the man is taking off work to fly up here and chauffeur me all way the home."

"It's probably going to be a while before Hunt lets you out of his sight again," Annie warned with a snicker. "Good thing you like each other."

Seneca stopped in her tracks when she saw the gathering of people in the meeting space of the shop. They clapped and sang out, "Surprise!" She turned to Annie and Alice. "Oooh, you two are sneaky!"

"Peggy's mostly to blame," Alice told her primly.

The waitress rushed up to give Seneca a hug. "Guilty as

charged. It was the least I could do after you gave me the chance to be part of a real crime investigation. We haven't had this much excitement ... well, since one of Annie's mysteries!" When Chief Edwards had shown Peggy a mug shot of the man Ian had tackled, she identified him as one of the two men Annie and Alice had seen in the diner.

Kate chimed in, "I just realized. Annie's mysteries usually start in her attic. Seneca's *ended* there!" The women laughed and guided their guest of honor to a table adorned with refreshments and a gift basket.

Peggy pointed at the basket. "Everyone added something for your new crochet hobby. We hope it will keep you busy for a while, and that you'll think of us."

Seneca looked around at the small group of women. "You are all amazing! Hunt and I are definitely going to come back for a visit next year." She winked at Annie and Alice. "We promise to leave the thugs in Texas, though."

Mary Beth raised a glass of punch. "I'll drink to that!"

After mingling with the tight-knit group, saying her thanks and goodbyes, Seneca returned with Annie and Alice to Grey Gables. Ian had volunteered to pick Hunt up from the Jetport so the surprise party would not be interrupted. The men were ensconced in two of the wicker porch chairs when the three women arrived, and Ian's sedan was parked behind Seneca's car.

"Hunt!" Seneca jumped from the car as soon as Annie had stopped, rushing to her husband. Hunt, of average height but with an air of power about him, caught his wife up in his arms, lifting her off her feet.

"It's been too quiet without you, Sen," Hunt murmured

against Seneca's cheek before setting his wife back on her feet. He nodded at Annie. "Thanks, Annie, for helping your unexpected visitor."

Annie hugged her old friend, enjoying the sight of the couple together again. Chief Edwards had collected enough evidence from Peggy, Alice, and the stolen license plate reported in Freeport to pressure Jonno Neff, the inexperienced thug Ian had tackled. He had collapsed under Ridge and Reed's questioning, giving evidence against both his partner and Alaso. The Marchals' happily-ever-after was looking more possible. As was Annie's and Ian's.

A while later, Seneca and Hunt drove away with windows down and hands waving, a six-pack of Moxie soda stowed in the backseat. Alice grinned at her two friends. "Well, I think it's time for me to head home. Annie, call me later about getting back to Pammy's class this week. See ya!" She disappeared between the hedges, whistling.

Annie and Ian relaxed in the wicker chairs, holding hands. It had been some time since she had felt so settled and serene. She finally knew in every part of her being that this was right; this was worth risking her heart.

"Ian," she began, looking deeply into his eyes, "I think I finally get why you always chastened me when I was delving into some mystery and getting myself into some pretty sticky—OK, dangerous—spots."

"Really?"

"Yes. It was about the time you were capturing a pistol-toting bad guy, who was bent on hurting my friend and me." Annie took a deep breath. "I know now how afraid you were all of those times my mysteries put me in danger. And I know why. You love me. It's as simple as that. I realized as you were strong-arming that hood, that you could have easily been hurt—or killed. At first I was angry, and then I was scared. And then it leaped out at me the way the leopard leaped out of my window. I was angry and scared because ... well ... I love you too."

"I probably wasn't in as much danger as Quill and Ridge."

"I'm grateful for what they did, but it's not the same."

"You know, when you told me Ridge had sent you those flowers as part of the scheme to get Seneca the photos, and I read the card, I did feel ever so slightly what might be considered jealous." Ian looked down at their entwined hands. "Ridge might be considered handsome by the ladies."

"Maybe so," said Annie. "But he has one tragic flaw."

"Oh? What's that?"

Annie leaned closer, kissed Ian warmly, and then laid her free hand against his cheek. "He's not you."